THEY
CANCELED
THE
DJ

To Maddi;

Write the story!
And thank you :)

Freddy
Kruz

THEY CANCELED THE DJ

A NOVEL BY
FREDDY CRUZ

EAST 26TH
PUBLISHING

HOUSTON

CHAPTER 1

I hate crowded malls, but mall smell makes my toes curl. The scent of new clothes, sneakers, food, and expensive perfume fuse together to form a veritable aromatic aphrodisiac. A hypnotic scent that strikes me and unsuspecting shoppers at Lecnac Grove Mall with the smell of American capitalism. The babble of hundreds of voices reminds me of the whirring sound of a seashell pressed to your ear. The shrieking of a random toddler's voice interrupts the otherwise peaceful ambient noise.

Guys like me, we enjoy days like this. Days when we radio DJs can bask in the spotlight of a grand-prize giveaway. Where radio listeners gather for the chance to win a grand prize. The old adage "many will try but few will win" holds true today. Tens of thousands of texts from office workers blowing off their conference calls and Zoom meetings. Delivery drivers pulling over at some random parking lot while their customer's food grows cold and stale. College students skipping class, huddled in their dorm rooms, listening impatiently for keywords to text. Stay-at-home parents letting their babies marinate in soiled diapers for an extra few minutes because an obscene number of free shoes is totally worth it. And today, my station, Nexus Radio, will give away twenty-thousand dollars' worth.

"AC!" a voice calls to my left. A short brunette waves at me, revealing a tattoo that snakes along the inside of her forearm. She's flanked by two kids wearing matching "My Mommy Rocks" T-shirts. "I thought that was you."

She approaches, dragging the two little stinkers by the wrist, their mouths outlined in blue from the cotton candy they're holding. They wave the white wands of cavity-inducing confection about, their eyes transfixed on the little indigo puff at the tip.

"Hey."

"I called your show last week. I'm Judy the HR lady," she says.

"Yeah, I remember you."

In my experience, when someone says, "I remember you," they don't remember you. But most of the time, I actually remember. My points of reference generally include scent—if unpleasant—and voice. Especially if said voice is abnormally raspy, like that of someone who smokes three packs of cigarettes a day and sounds like a serial killer on the phone.

"You're still the adult in the office?" I ask.

"Duh." Judy winks. Her laugh is interrupted by a cough that sounds so painful it burns my chest. "Adults in the office don't get trashed at company parties and end up with accidental face tats."

We share a laugh, snap a selfie, and I continue on my way. Past an overpriced dress shop with the judgy mannequin staring a hole in me. Past a calendar booth with a thousand different types of calendars, mostly of the canine variety. Past a greeting card store with oversized plush animals in the window—nothing says "I'm a try-hard who's only out for one thing" quite like a $250 koala wearing a T-shirt that reads "You are koalified to hug me."

Getting to meet Nexus listeners who call into my show feels a lot like meeting a long-lost relative. Speaking on the phone, texting, tweeting, and commenting on Instagram posts is one thing. Sharing hugs and high fives in person is another. And spending five hours a day, every week, in a padded room is enough to make even the most antisocial radio personality change their ways. Especially after a pandemic.

As I stroll through the forest of families, strollers, shoppers, and oversized shopping bags, a train crosses in front of me.

Chooooo-chooooo!

The rainbow-colored cash cow on wheels with a white foam cloud atop the engine chugs along. Screaming little humans powder the seats next to begrudging parents. Mostly dads. Their soulless eyes, mapped with lines of red from sleep deprivation, stare forward in a trance while their mouths remain gaped slightly open, waiting for someone to insert the barrel of a gun. Their once-clean college shirt, now tagged with the toddler graffiti of fruit punch, is their white flag of surrender.

"Hear that?" I ask the lady next to me. College age, perhaps. Wearing a ball cap with a braid bleeding downward out the back, yoga pants, and a baseball-style jersey with pop star River Bronswell's face on it. Once considered "the poor man's Shawn Mendes," River catapulted into superstardom with his single "Dead Inside." And now, he's unavoidable.

Rumor has it that seals and penguins are more likely to avoid certain death at the hands of polar bears if the stations in Antarctica play him nonstop. But I digress.

Chooooo-chooooo!

She raises an eyebrow at me. "The screaming? Yes, unfortunately."

I wag a forefinger in disagreement. "Wrong. Birth control."

She smiles and laughs as it takes a moment to understand what I mean. Her laugh reveals the most perfect dimples. Dimples I've declared —to myself—that I must see in an environment outside of work. Like, a date or two. Or ten thousand.

My dad's a doctor. One day at brunch, the old man and I had our eyes on the same woman. A dimpled dame wearing tight jeans and a shirt that read "Nobody Cares, Work Harder." "When the zygomaticus major is shorter than normal," he said to me with a mouthful of smoked salmon, "you get the precious crater we call the dimple."

"Your zygomaticus major pulls well," I say.

She wrinkles her nose and rears her head back.

"Your dimples. I...I like your dimples."

The wailing wah-wah express interrupts the uncomfortable silence that sullied my well-intentioned compliment.

I clear my throat. "Here comes another sound," I say with a hand cupped to my ear. "The sound of ten dollars getting flushed down the toilet."

The train passes and the security guard lets us through. She rushes away.

"You here for the shopping spree?" I ask.

She stops and turns. Smiling, she answers, "Yeah. I am."

Good. Plenty of time for me to make up for this painfully weird exchange. Can't have people thinking that AC lacks social skills. I grin. "Me, too."

"Hey, you're that AC guy from Nexus, right?"

"I've been called worse. What should I call you?"

"Bobbi. With an 'i.'"

I hold back a giggle and bite my tongue, stifling my involuntary urge to blurt out the first thing to come to mind. Something one of my old neighbors once said. "Women whose names begin with 'b' and end with 'i' tend to be strippers. Bobbi, Brandi, Bambi, Britni, Bibi, so on and so forth."

Shoppers' bags bounce off my legs as we navigate the jungle of consumerism. A tiny old lady springs up from a massage chair amidst the sea of frantic shoppers and shoves a flyer in my face. "Gee, thanks," I say to the lady, who by now has walked back to her table next to her chair. "Care for an overpriced massage on a raggedy chair?" I ask Bobbi with a wink as I fold it up and put it into my back pocket.

"You might not remember this, but—"

I remember exactly where this is going because her voice sounds familiar. So I run interference. "Nice River Bronswell top. You going to his show this summer?"

"If I do, it'd be the tenth time I saw him," she answers.

"Wow, mildly obsessed," I say. My eyes squint. I stop walking and she does, too. Lowering my head, I scan my eyes from side to side and lean in, asking, "You're not on any watch lists, are you?"

Bobbi stiffens. Her eyebrows arch up and her mouth opens.

Something tells me I crossed a line. "Okay, no watch lists."

"As I was saying," she says in a don't-you-dare-interrupt-me-again manner. "We talked for a couple of minutes last month."

I bite down on the lower corner of my lip and stare away in anticipation of her next comment.

"You said the hardest thing about playing a River Bronswell song on Nexus Radio was making sure his fans could finish cleaning the litter boxes for their eleven cats before it ends."

Diarrhea of the mouth, incoming. "To be fair, you look like you only own seven."

Not everybody likes my sense of humor. But luckily, Bobbi play-slaps my arm and reaches inside her purse. "Mind if we snap a pic?"

"Without me? Rude!" shouts a raspy voice. It belongs to another woman of about the same age. Slightly taller with a larger-than-normal smile and blinding white teeth. She, too, is wearing a River Bronswell top. It reads, "I like River Bronswell, donuts, and maybe two other people." Her blue hair and bangs remind me of the kind of gal who in

2020 would have accused a six-year-old boy of trying to kill her if his mask wasn't covering his nose. Definitely my best bro Cade's type. And now, I can already see us on a double date. If I don't make this even more awkward.

"There you are," says Bobbi. She motions toward me. "This is that AC guy from Nexus Radio."

"Lyla," she says, extending a hand. "Lyla Stanton. I don't really listen to the radio, but nice to meet you."

I return the gesture and say, "Well, I'm happy your friend does."

"Me, too," replies Bobbi, offering a fist bump to Lyla. "'Cuz we might be winning us a bunch of shoes." They make the universal symbol for an exploding fist bump.

They share a giddy giggle. Bobbi shoves an elbow into my side. "Wish me luck?"

Someone wish me luck. I'll need it if I want her number, and my breakfast has quickly turned into a DEFCON-1-level halitosis catastrophe.

Protip: Never eat onions before working at a large event if you tend to forget breath mints.

"We gonna snap that picture or not?" she asks as we approach the Nexus Radio booth in front of the Neat Feet Boutique.

"Right, of course," I reply, cupping a hand over my mouth and exhaling into it, then sniffing for bad breath. Not ideal. But at least it didn't make me faint.

Bobbi swings an arm around my waist and another around Lyla's neck. She yanks me toward her as I place an arm around her shoulder. Any other time, the sweat seeping out of my pores, through my fingers, and down the palm of the hand on top of her T-shirt would have me worried. But after feeling her hand slide slowly off my waist to unwrap her arm, not so much. "Cute!" she exclaims, looking at her smartphone.

"Use a filter on me. I'm not wearing enough foundation," says Lyla, unimpressed.

Bobbi scoffs as she shoves her smartphone into her purse. "Whatever, you're flawless as always."

"Both of you are," I say with a thumb in the air. "After this is over, we can share makeup tips and put them on Tik Tok."

They reply with a blank stare.

A line starts to form around the Nexus Radio booth, listeners participating in one of Lecnac Grove Mall's biggest contests of the year. "I'll leave you two to decide between Juno and Clarendon," I say. "But if you want my professional selfie opinion, always go with no filter."

Bobbi tosses me a coltish side-eye. "Yeah, what he said. He's the professional, after all."

The Nexus Radio staff, led by Darby Winston, greets me with a mic and clipboard. The team calls her the resident firecracker. The getter of shit that needs to get done. I call her my fourth favorite redhead, right behind Ed Sheeran, Wendy, and Carrot Top. I pay attention to her instructions like a sleep-deprived high schooler pays attention in first period chemistry...I don't. "Then you have to *blah blah blah*." Not because I'm some spoiled, know-it-all radio personality who's only working the event for the extra money and free food afterward. But because every time I look up to greet a friendly face, I'm met by the hugest brown eyes and dimples. Bobbi's.

My stomach twists, and I'm not sure if it's because of my breakfast or Bobbi—hopefully, it's the latter. It twists like the first time I set foot in the control room of a radio station. The rows of blinking lights, the volume needles, the microphones. The five computer monitors. The multiple clocks. Clocks that count up. Clocks that count down. It was like a spaceship I never thought I'd learn to fly. The equipment was intimidating. Bobbi's intimidating.

And she has me zygo-hooked.

CHAPTER 2

N o matter where you go, radio station events are the same.

Bedazzle a place with rollaway banner made of cheap plastic. Set up a booth, which is really a rickety table. Lay a crusty, nylon blend cover on top with the station logo in front, speckled with black and brown. Forget the fact that those dots are bacteria and mold waiting to latch on to some poor kid who only wants to spin our decrepit wheel for some prize that Mom and Dad will undoubtedly toss in the trash when little Junior's not looking. The *real* prize is going to the prize table and leaving without a staph infection.

Play cornhole. Win a T-shirt that only took seven hundred gallons of water to make in some Third World country. Different locations, same crowd. Every single time.

The "I won't ever listen to this station again" car salesman who wanted tickets but didn't get them is the same as the "your station's dead to me" wireless phone store manager who wanted the last T-shirt but didn't get it.

But not Nexus radio events.

They're actual events with prizes people want, like the $20,000 shoe spree at Neat Feet Boutique. Twenty listeners. One winner. One shopping spree. And all they have to do is play a slot machine. No wheel with duct tape holding it together, instilling in us the fear that a draft of wind will knock it over and crush someone's foot. No cornhole with musty beanbags laced with the dust of radio promotions past. Nexus has a Vegas-style slot machine with *boopity-zingitty* sounds and DJs' faces on the reels. Listener after listener spins the reels on the slot machine. They pull the lever and push the buttons. The crowd howls as the next contestant prances toward me, a listener with bouncy curls dyed hot pink.

"And our next contestant is..."

I swing the mic in her direction, careful not to jam it into her face. Can't have anyone suing the station for seventy-five trillion dollars in damages for destroying a listener's teeth.

"Mercedes."

I remember the name. Frequent caller.

Our VIP listener whips her curls back, leans in close, and whisper-asks, "Are you wondering what I had for lunch?"

Call me perpetually hangry. Tell me I'm in love with food. I don't care, but I always have to know what people are eating. Last week, Mercedes made my day—she called into the show and told me she was having a peanut butter and jelly sandwich but prefers creamy peanut butter because she doesn't like nuts in her mouth. "Mercedes is hungry for victory today," I say, ignoring her suggestive tone.

Mercedes rubs her hands together and pulls the lever. She scores fifty points.

Darby walks up. She lifts her clipboard to her face. I wanna lift a breath mint to her mouth. "We're down to our final three contestants and need a winner asap. This lady's name is—"

"Bobbi!" I exclaim.

Bobbi joins me at the slot machine, and all I can think is how I should have asked her for her number before the contest. What if she leaves before I have a chance to ask and my only means of connecting is the ever-so-creepy DM slide? Or maybe I can ask an intern to fetch her number for me. Less creep factor, right? Or how about following her on Instagram? Not creepy, as long as I don't go and start liking posts from 2014. All these thoughts run through my head, until Darby smacks me on the back with her clipboard.

"Bobbi's another proud Nexus Radio listener and a huge River Bronswell fan," I declare. "My guess is that he's your lucky charm today?"

"No, and neither are any of the eleven cats you accused me of having."

Touché.

The zygomaticus masterpiece herself manhandles the slot machine, giving it some extra muscle. A good spin is a long spin, which means more time to focus on the craters of beauty nestled in her porcelain skin.

"Since Bobbi gave our wheel a three-year-long spin, we may as well make ourselves acquainted," I say to the crowd with a game-show smile. "So, where were you when you called in to qualify for the shopping spree?"

"At work. I'm a masseuse with the best hands in the Western Hemisphere," she answers, wiggling her fingers in the air. Then she inserts a hand in her back pocket and digs out a business card holder. She opens it and slides me a shiny, pink card.

I wanna kiss the card and scream "Thank you!" to the universe for giving me the signal I was hoping for, but I shove it in my back pocket instead. "Well, you laid 'em nice-n-heavy on our slot machine, let's see your score."

Bobbi grabs the mic from my hand. I hope this is the part where she saves me the effort and asks me out to dinner. "Aren't you gonna ask me about my other job?"

"Seeing as how your spin won't end for another year, sure," I reply, motioning for her to return the mic.

Her caramel brown eyes light up. They match the freckles on her face. She leans in and says, "I moonlight as a River Bronswell fan fiction author." Lifting a hand to her ear, she asks the crowd, "Any River fans in the house today?"

She's met with screeches and squeals.

Maybe she does have eleven cats.

"Well, since the wheel's still spinning. Where can we find your work?"

"Follow me on WattPad, username RiversFavoriteAuthor," she replies.

"I look forward to the movie version of the book," I say with a wink.

She nods. "Thank you," she says. "But remember, the book is always better than the movie."

The reels slow to a stop. Some listeners cover their mouths in anticipation, others turn away because they can't stand the suspense. The first reel lands on Biggs, he's worth a hundred points. The second reel lands on Sasha, she's worth another hundred. A chorus of "woos" permeates the store.

"Let's go Bobbi!" shouts Lyla from afar.

The third reel lands on the Nexus logo.

"Three hundred for the Nexus logo, plus Biggs and Sasha at a hundred points apiece puts you at five hundred!" I shout.

"I won!" shouts Bobbi, reaching out toward Lyla. The two exchange a Super Bowl–worthy hug. The only thing missing is a Gatorade shower and television reporter asking them where they could possibly go after winning a shoe spree from the illustrious Nexus Radio, and then they say, "We're going to Disney World!"

What's left of my focus shrivels away after the end of the contest. And the moment Darby and the promotions crew motion me toward Bobbi and Lyla, my bowels go full Benedict Arnold, betraying me before legions of Nexus Radio listeners.

A rumbling. A gurgle. A beast claws at the inside my stomach. I can't see my face, but it has to be whiter than the porcelain god waiting for me to bend the knee. The beast, whatever it is, slithers and squirms around my insides. It grips the pipes that are my intestines and strangles them with unforgiving force.

But I'm a professional. I shake it off and approach Bobbi for a picture, hoping our digital team can filter it so I don't look like the Grim Reaper's new bestie. Everything teeters and totters.

"Congratulations," I say, lifting a sweaty hand to shake Bobbi's.

She flashes me a smile. The fury of my last meal keeps me from returning the favor. The spiciest breakfast tacos I've ever eaten rage up my throat, out my mouth, and all over her shoes.

A symphony of screams, moans, and sighs fills the air. I collapse to a knee. The palm of my hand skids on the regurgitated goop. My chest smacks the floor, and my cheek splashes into a pile of bile.

Bobbi dashes for a nearby bench, conveniently located next to the cash register. She examines her feet and the rest of her legs to see if more of my breakfast landed on her. An employee sets a can of Lysol and paper towels next to her. Lyla wraps her hand and forearm with the paper towels to form a makeshift glove and sprays half the can on it. The hissing sound reminds me of a deflating balloon. A metaphor for my deflated ego.

Bobbi peeks around Lyla. With the back of her hand at her mouth, she yells, "Good thing I just won a crapload of free shoes!" Then she holds out a thumb and nods. At me. And this can only mean one thing. I might just stand a chance if I can escape without any further incident.

The store manager shouts, "Someone grab a mop!"

An onlooker shouts, "Dude, this is going on the internet."

Their voices are pitched down like drunken versions of an outer space movie villain. They find my lack of intestinal control disturbing.

The world around me spins like a funhouse tunnel, a vortex of vomit. I roll over on my back. The cold puddle of putrid tacos colonizes my Nexus Radio polo, seeping through to my skin. Blurred faces hover over me as I try to regain balance.

I try to catch a glimpse of Bobbi, but Lyla blocks my view and my stomach twists around, knocking me back to the ground.

A voice calls for a paramedic.

Another voice, a nightmarish version of Darby's, calls for everyone to calm down.

I roll over onto my stomach, army crawling through my sludge. I am a Zamboni of barftastical proportions, smoothing out the floor of the Neat Feet Boutique on my way to the men's bathroom as a chorus of unintelligible voices floods my ears.

CHAPTER 3

My parents gross me out. Yeah, yeah, quite a statement coming from the guy who hurled all over a woman's shoes. Seriously, though. Trading sloppy kisses at a restaurant and rubbing their hands all over each other's backs makes me wanna call them an Uber and send them to the nearest motel.

Dad pops the lime out of his bottle of Corona, squeezes the juice in, and rubs it around the top before wrapping it in a bar napkin. "You've never really had luck with women."

"Gee, thanks," I reply.

The table jostles upward. Water splashes out of my glass. His eyes widen and he shrugs, as if what he said is an undeniable fact of life and his tone wasn't at all judgy.

Mom scoffs and bobs her head sideways in my direction. "Do you have any idea what our boy has just gone through?"

Dad sips his beer. A lone piece of lime clings to his mustache for life. "I do," he replies. "Which is why I tried to convince you to have him meet us where they don't sell Mexican food. And you don't have to stomp on my foot. These boots are brand new, ya know."

"I'm okay now, guys," I say.

Except for the fact that I made a fool out of myself in front of my listeners and my coworkers. And I hurled all over some woman's shoes. A woman I was hoping to go on a date with. A woman who, despite our weird exchange, gave me her business card. Maybe because she's an assertive entrepreneurial type who hands business cards to everyone she meets. But she handed her card to me—in front of all those people. That means something, I think. I...hope. I still have her business card. Sure, it got a little gunk on it from the Incident, but I washed it with soap and water. And thankfully, the card is glossy, so the ink didn't smudge. And if you have to know, I gave it a ten-second spritz of Lysol to kill 99.9 percent of the germs.

Mom reaches for Dad's mustache, and he jerks his head away. "Remember that one time you broke your finger after that girl said she'd go with you to the sixth-grade dance?" He takes another swig. "You fell off your bike after hopping a curb!" He guzzles down the rest of his brew.

Mom play-slaps my arm. "I remember that!"

Me, too. An unfortunate reminder that I've been doomed to horrible experiences with the opposite sex since I was tweenage brat. A broken pinky here. A couple of bad dates there. And a viral incident in front of a hundred or so people armed with cameras on their phones to solidify my place in Cupid's Hall of Shame.

"So, Mom," I say with a hint of aggression, my attempt to change the subject. "Save any animals at the hospital today?"

Dad bellows with laughter. He raises his napkin to his mouth, and it's about damn time that piece of lime unlatched itself from the crevices of his caterpillar-like flavor saver. "That reminds me, remember AC's fling with that one intern of yours, Maria?"

Mom coughs and spits out a splash of margarita. "My goodness. Stop it, won't you!" She smears her napkin across her lip and holds it up to her mouth for longer than a few seconds. I see her shoulders jolt up and down. My own mother laughs at my misfortune. "We found out the hard way that you're allergic to cats, didn't we, son?"

"You thought your eyes were gonna fall out, they were so swollen," says Dad.

The two laugh. Loudly. We're that table at the restaurant. As soon as heads turn our way, they stop. Their eyes meet. My dad's eyes sag like a puppy dog's, and he leans in for a peck on her cheek.

"Are the two of you done?"

"Papa," Mom says with a hint of guilt in her voice. "We're not trying to make fun of you."

"Well, you're doing a bang-up job of it," I reply as my eyes wander upward. They make contact with a donkey piñata wearing a T-shirt that reads, "Save water, drink tequila." I could go for a shot or seven, actually.

My phone buzzes. I leave it alone, face down on the table. Mom and dad look at me, then my phone. It buzzes again.

"You gonna answer that?" asks Dad.

I bow my head down and squeeze my eyes shut.

"Son," says Mom.

"Ten years ago, you both would have yelled at me and threatened to take my phone away if I even looked at it during dinner," I say. "And now you want me to pick it up?'"

"Might be work," says Dad, as he lifts his near empty bottle for one last sip.

"Okay, okay, okay," I growl.

I pick it up and press my thumb down to unlock the screen. Cade. *"The morning show wants you to go on the air with them on Monday to talk about what happened at Neat Feet lol. 8am sharp. Get there a few minutes early. You know how they are."*

Great. Because reliving that moment is just what I need to kickstart my week. I shake my phone because the donkey appears to be laughing at me, and shaking it will keep me from hurling it at the donkey's pathetic face.

"Could your face get any redder?" asks Dad. He shakes his head, lifts his empty bottle, and calls out to our waiter. "Another round, *por favor*?"

"Cade," I mumble, holding up my phone.

"Such a sweetheart," says Mom with a grin.

A sweetheart with a sweet spot for making my life a living hell. My fingers slam down onto the screen of my phone. *"Are you kidding me? I'm trying to FORGET what happened this weekend!"*

"Yeah, he's cool," I answer. "Except when he conveniently acts like my boss when I need him to be my friend."

"Which is why you should never mix business with pleasure," says Dad, wagging a finger in the air.

Mom agrees, nodding her head. "At face value, it makes sense to be close with the people you spend a third of your day with." She lifts her margarita glass to her mouth to fish out a chunk of ice. Between chomps, she says, "But why on earth would you want to spend any more time than necessary with people you're cooped up with them in the same, drab, fluorescent lit office suite?"

"Yes," slurs Dad. Mom's definitely driving home tonight. "They talk behind your back, steal your lunch from the office fridge, smell up the restroom, and, if you're lucky," he stops to gulp down a long sip of beer. "If you're lucky, you're only subjected to fewer than ten meetings with them per week."

I tune them out.

Cade hits me with another message. *"We don't really have a choice here, dude."*

I don't get the *we* in his response. He wasn't even there. What is this *we*? *We* didn't throw up on a woman's shoes. *We* didn't crawl in agony to the men's room of an overpriced shoe store while people filmed. *We* didn't wash the stink of regurgitated food out of a staff shirt with cheap industrial soap. *We* didn't leave the mall through an employee exit to avoid human interaction. *We* didn't spend five hours on Twitter, Instagram, and Facebook looking at posts and comments and leaving 694 nasty replies in a Twitter draft folder. I did.

"What the—"

I catch myself before saying *fuck* in front of my parents. Decorum, you know. It means something in a world where more and more kids, young and old, talk in front of and to their parents as if they're drunken roommates.

My fingers pound my phone again. *"What do you mean, we?"*

"Look at him," says Dad, pointing a salsa-laden tortilla chip at me. "He's mad. And he's gotta spend forty-plus hours with Cade every week. And he actually gets along with his boss."

Not at this moment.

Cade fires another message. *Biggs and Sasha sent me AND Lilian a message, talking about how amazing it would be to make a bit out of what happened to you.*

Yes, totally amazing.

He sends me another message. *And you know that when they send Lilian a message, that means we don't get a say in the matter.*

Ahh, yes. The old "sic the boss's boss in on our request so you have to bend the knee and to our morning show monarchy."

"What happened?" asks Mom.

"The morning show wants me to talk about—" I make quotation marks with my fingers. "*The incident* at the shoe giveaway."

"Awesome," she replies.

Dad roars with laughter. "I thought *I* was the drunk one, amor." He plunges his head down into his forearm.

"Awesome is the last word that comes to mind," I say, refusing to subscribe to her belief in cognitive reframing. Sure, changing the way we see things makes sense on paper. Referring to them as "awesome" gives us a new and better starting point—until it's time to practice this exercise in real life. Because referring to a shitty incident as "awesome" is next to impossible when sulking in misery is so much more convenient. But Mom's good at it. Like one year in high school, when I didn't make the football team, she said it was awesome because she didn't want her boy to get hurt and one day get hit by those three-hundred-pound cornfed boys and have to eat through a straw for the rest of my life.

"What's her name?" Mom asks.

I smile at the thought of her name. "Bobbi," I say.

Mom taps a forefinger on her lips.

"Bobbi Falstaff," I continue. Owner of the Den of Zen.

"It'd be awesome if Ms. Falstaff happened to hear my son on the Biggs and Sasha Show this Mon—"

"Here we go," I interrupt.

Dad lugs his drunken head from his arm. "Let...your mom finish talking...boy."

"Sorry, Mom," I mumble, bobbing my head from side to side. "As you were saying?"

No amount of cognitive reframing and positive thinking could possibly dig me out of the annals of internet shame.

"All I'm saying is, AC," says mom. She wraps an arm around Dad's neck and tugs him toward her. His cheek curls up, and his lips pucker into her armpit as she continues, "This clown followed me in a dark parking lot at nine o'clock in the evening and asked me for my number." She rubs her knuckles into his wavy hair. "And if that worked for him, then maybe you've got a chance."

I hope she's right.

CHAPTER 4

Books don't consume my life. Not completely, anyway. But I
love books. And I agree with Bobbi: the book will always be
better than the movie. Especially if we're talking about *Fight Club* and
The Hunger Games. No amount of Brad Pitt and Jennifer Lawrence could
ever change that. And until now, my discriminating taste has all but
banished the world of fan fiction.

I nestle myself into bed and flap open my e-reader and search for
@RiversFavoriteAuthor. Biggs would say the typing of those words
alone knocks my testosterone down a few hundred notches. But I know
that an extensive reconnaissance mission can win me favor in the
battlefield of dating. No matter how strange said mission is.

There she is, @RiversFavoriteAuthor, aka Bobbi. Her profile pic
shows her seated in a red satin chair, in front of a fireplace surrounded by
a huge bookshelf. In her left hand, she holds a pen with shiny gold cap.
The palm of her right hand cups her cheek. She doesn't look into the
camera but instead focuses her attention on a bright green notebook,

which accentuates her forest green and white polka-dotted skirt with hot pink sweater. She looks more like a historian than a fan-fiction author.

I tap on her current work, *The Day River Played Me Like a Ukelele*. The cover shows a digitally drawn, shirtless River Bronswell holding a bikini-clad brunette. In his arms, she strokes a strategically placed ukulele in front of his crotch. It has over three hundred thousand reads and nearly eight thousand likes. Impressive.

I tap to read.

The mere sight of River Bronswell makes me throb down there. My fingers dance along my thighs and between them, as I watch his fingers diddle his ukelele. High definition, 4k hotness permeates the ninety-inch screen in my studio. He looks down upon me as I writhe around in joyful pain on my massage table. "Take me, Mr. Bronswell. Take me and strum my parts harder than your Fender."

One paragraph in and *RiversFavoriteAuthor* on WattPad has me needing a cold shower. Stat. Now I'm convinced she has eleven cats—maybe more.

My mind tells me to catch some z's before my forced guest appearance on Nexus Radio's *Biggs and Sasha Show*. My heart tells me to continue reading more of Bobbi's latest work of fan fic.

I set my e-reader down on the nightstand, next to my alarm clock. My phone buzzes. Opting for the dopamine hit of an Instagram notification, I pick it up and slide my thumb over the button to open the app. *Ignore the notifications. Ignore the tags. Ignore the viral incident. Just see who followed you.*

"Hmph," I grumble. "RiversFavoriteAuthor just followed you."

She followed me. The guy who yacked all over her shoes in front of a bunch of people.

I sit up and fling the sheets off. Swinging my feet to the side and onto the floor, I run a hand through my hair. Then a thumb and forefinger across my eyes.

What do I do? Follow her back? Duh. Of course I should follow her back. But when? Clearly, I shouldn't do the desperate thing and follow her back right now? Right? I set my phone down on my chest and gaze up at the ceiling fan. Maybe it'll hypnotize me into making the right decision.

I tap on her profile, careful not to click on her InstaStory. Can't have her knowing about my Instacreeping her footprint.

My phone buzzes again. A new direct message. From her.

Screw it. I smash the follow button and open up the message.

Great to meet you today!

Nice. It's almost as if she forgot about what happened to her feet. As if she forgot about my sliding down the aisle of Neat Feet Boutique in a pile of my own sludge. I fall back into bed. "Think before you type, AC," I whisper to myself. "The internet's forever and screenshots are a thing." Not that I plan to send her a scandalous message or compromising pic of myself. Lord knows, she probably deals with more than her fair share of pics of the eggplant variety, if you know what I mean. And I'm sure you do.

Great to meet you, too, I type.

She read it. Now my phone shows her typing. The dots move, teasing me. Luring me into thinking that she'll do the hard work and ask me out.

She replies. *How's your tummy?*

Tummy. How motherly. Maybe she's trolling me. Or maybe she isn't. I have to let her know my bowels can withstand even the most wretched tacos.

Feeling well enough to read your story on WattPad.

She sends me a blushing face emoji. I send her a shocked face emoji. She replies with a crying laughing face emoji.

I type, *Giving E. L. James a run for her money, I see.*

Then she replies with, *Nexus Radio plays Cardi B, quit acting like a church lady.*

Touché.

I laugh as I set my phone back down on the nightstand. Then it buzzes again. *So glad we got to meet.*

Me too, I reply.

Before I can power down my phone, it buzzes again. Another DM from Bobbi. *Btw, ignore the internet nobodies.*

What does she know that I don't?

Until now, I did a bang-up job of doing just that. Ignoring them. Not feeding them. Not even thinking about them. But sometimes, all it takes is the right message at the right time—which is actually the wrong message at the wrong time—to goad you into seeking out the very thing people tell you not to seek out.

I close out of Instagram and open up Twitter with the press of a thumb.

Until now, listening to Cade and Biggs and Sasha and Mom and Dad worked. The phone stayed off and away for most of the weekend. Social media was off limits. No Facebook, no Twitter, no Instagram. No kids using the sounds of my sickness to create TikTok videos with laugh tracks and graphics of the graphic display. And no Clubhouse meet-ups among radio colleagues to discuss "what to do if one of your high-profile personalities goes viral for all the wrong reasons."

Until now. Because the reality is, I can't escape from the secret-sauce-looking gunk that painted the floor of the Neat Feet Boutique. No running from the chunks of failure that spawned internet fame. I click. I scroll. Nothing but my bile plastered over all the local news sites.

Headline: Local resident wins big, DJ loses his lunch

Headline: Nexus DJ known for hurling hits, hurls all over woman

Gone are the days of wondering how viral failures feel after achieving fifteen minutes of shame.

"Great. I'm viral in Italy," I mumble.

Headline: I annunciatore vomita sulla folla di donne lo perde

I grab my smartphone, hoping Twitter can give me something other than a 360-degree view of the infamous regurgitation.

I'm tagged more times than I can count.

My stomach is a twisted pretzel of pain. The overactive air conditioner hums loudly above my bed as I seek refuge in my sheets.

Headline: DJ hosts shoe shopping spree, pukes on woman's shoes

This video has 101,302 likes, 47,926 retweets, and 10,721 comments.

Some internet guru once wrote, "Don't feed the trolls, no matter how hungry they are."

My thumb slides up and down my smartphone, my most loyal companion over the last couple of days.

He should change his name to Pepe Le Puke, tweets @muzikstan21.

Don't.

Someone buy him a bottle of Pepto DISMAL bahahaha, tweets @seymourjugz with a .GIF of Woody Harrelson blowing chunks into a toilet.

Feed.

AC, captain of Project: I'll puke on you, replies @muzikstan21 with a .GIF of Peter Griffin from *Family Guy* hurling in his living room.

The.

It ain't easy being queazy, tweets @seymourjugz.

Trolls.

Shakespeare is to bard, what AC is to barf, tweets @muzikstan21. *And someone cancel his show before he does this again.*

My blood boils, and engaging my rage appears to be the only thing that can cool it down. I stop, close my eyes, and think of my mom's silly little reframing exercise. And I remember something Mom always says. "Awesome," I whisper.

Realizing there are only so many hours in the day and so much energy to bestow upon the lowest of the internet ranks, I narrow my list. "Nice profile pic," I mumble, scanning @muzikstan21's Twitter feed for fuel to ignite my act of virtual vengeance. The picture is of a twenty-something guy standing next to a sickly looking elderly woman in a 1970s-style rocker. His bio reads: *Killing the world with 1,000 kinds of kindness. No time for hate. Fluent in humility.*

My eyeballs roll into the back of my brain. This from the guy who wants my show canceled.

"Awesome," I mumble again. I type the words *"your life is nothing more than an accident, @muzikstan21."* Before I can hit the tweet button, I hit the backspace button fifty-seven times. Not because I have a beautiful soul but because he deserves more than a tweet. Something to restore order to the internet universe. And most importantly, my universe. Something that'll ruin him. Well, not completely ruin him. I don't want it to be a Hiroshima on his life, just a targeted drone strike.

I scroll through more tweets. *Too bad my dickhead boss won't let me see my sick and dying grandma. Her death will be on his conscience.*

My thumb continues to scroll and bingo. There's the tweet. *Happy hour with Plethora Plastics Inc. staff. #LivingOurBestLives*

I should ride the dopamine high of trading messages with Bobbi on Insta and let the oxytocin help me fantasize about being in one of her fan fiction stories in my sleep. But I opt for rage scrolling a douchebag's

Twitter feed and planning his demise. Which is so much better than tweeting at their employer or writing a stern Yelp review. That's for losers with no imagination. But before I finish plotting his downfall, I gotta catch some Zs. Make sure I'm rested for what'll definitely be the most painful appearance on the *Biggs and Sasha Show* ever.

CHAPTER 5

I like my life, love my job, and never dread Monday. But today is an exception.

All I want is to disappear. Not *disappear* disappear. Just vanish from the face of the earth for, I don't know—a long time. Long enough for the algorithms to bury the video of the Incident to the fiftieth page of a Google search. Or fifty-thousandth. Or long enough for Bobbi to forget about the Incident with just enough time to finish off that @Muzikstan21 idiot.

But that won't happen. Which is why I'd settle for a rerecording. Like when I'm recording commercials and if my pronunciation is off, I can always go back and rerecord. Slur a word? Rerecord. Fumble over a sentence? Rerecord. Mistime your sixty-second copy, and now it's sixty-two seconds? Rerecord. Get interrupted by a sales guy who has no idea what the bright red and white recording light outside the studio means? Rerecord. I'd rewind and stop right at the moment I poured habanero sauce on my tacos. Then I'd record over everything about that day. The bumbling exchanges, the weird jokes, the odd comment about Bobbi's dimples. And definitely the vomit part. I could hit rerecord and be the AC my listeners think I am. Smooth and confident. Then Bobbi and I could ride off into the sunset atop a rainbow-colored unicorn and lie on a beach, where I'd feed her chocolate-covered strawberries, and she could declare her love for me between bites.

But that won't happen either.

I pull the zipper of my hoodie all the way up to my neck, cross my arms, and dig my hands into my armpits. The gentle hum of the air conditioner vent in the control room serves as a reminder that when life is uncomfortable, it can always dial up the discomfort.

"I guess building management doesn't realize it's mid-July," I whine, yanking the hood over my head.

"Suck it up, buttercup," growls Sasha without moving her mouth. She then mouths the words "we're on" and points to her mic.

"The Nexus Radio $20,000 Shoe Shopping Spree is still trending on Twitter, and you'll find out why when our very own AC joins the show next," announces Biggs, the other half of the *Biggs and Sasha Show*.

They remove their headphones, turn to me in the next studio, and wave me in. "Vomit-nos, I mean...uh, *vaminos*, AC, we're gonna have fun with this," says Biggs.

Sasha snorts. She takes a swig of water from the bottle next to her but spits it out after Biggs fake wretches with a finger in his mouth. Wiping her pouty lips with a shirt sleeve, she says, "I was gonna bake you some cookies but didn't want you to toss them."

Biggs erupts in laughter, smacking the studio console.

"Ha, ha, ha," I reply, clapping my hands slowly.

Sasha grabs a makeup compact from her bag and licks her teeth. She sticks a pinky finger between her two front ones. She lowers the compact so she can make eye contact with me. "How are ya?"

I hold out a hand and make the universal gesture for "so-so." But that's a lie because "so-so" would be ten thousand times better than the past two days.

Biggs fixates on the monitor in front of him. He goes on and on about how I'm trending worldwide. How I'm world famous because I threw up on someone's shoes. "Bro, were the tacos that bad? No, scratch that. Do attractive females always make you socially incompetent?" He holds up a hand, scanning over his commercial log to make sure he's running the correct commercials and cross-references with the screen. "Hold that thought. We're on in less than a minute."

I can't help but wonder what they have planned for this segment. They wouldn't tell me. Not even a hint. "Can someone tell me what we're going to talk about?" I ask.

"Everything," they reply in unison.

I threw up on a woman's shoes and went viral on the internet. Not sure what else they want to discuss.

Sasha puts her headphones on. Biggs, too. They give me a skeptical stare. "Ready to roll in twenty seconds," he says. He points Sasha to her smartphone, hinting that he wants her to pick it up and take a glance at it.

I grab my headphones. The counter on the console's clock trudges as Father Time teases me with seconds that feel like hours.

Sasha removes one side of her headphones and holds her smartphone to me. "There's always more to the story, AC." She snaps the ear cover over her ear.

Sasha holds up a screenshot of the video from the event, showing me looking hopelessly desperate for attention from Bobbi, just moments before I regurgitated my lunch on her shoes.

I lose myself in my own fear for a moment when I'm interrupted by Biggs's pristine pipes.

"Welcome to Nexus Radio Mornings with Biggs and Sasha and a very special guest in studio."

Sasha twirls the spiral cord connected to her headphones and swings her feet, kicking off her sneakers. "This guy's responsible for making our radio station's $20,000 Shopping Spree trend worldwide through the weekend—please welcome our afternoon host, AC."

I'm never at a loss for words. Except for now.

"Hello...earth to AC," shouts Sasha, tapping her microphone, which makes four loud thuds.

"Oh, right. Hey."

Biggs cuts in to pick up my slack. "C'mon bro, spew the details."

Ha. Spew. This is why management pays them the big bucks. Make middle school jokes at my expense.

"I probably got sick from something I ate."

Biggs turns away and clicks the mouse to his side. He announces into his mic that he's going to play the exact moment that turned me into a worldwide failure. "This is what it sounded like when AC threw up all over a woman's shoes."

Biggs hits play. Werbly audio permeates the airwaves. He laughs as I watch the video for what has to be the thousandth time. "Well, Captain Regurgitator?" He fidgets with his mouse and stops the video. Thank God. "Did you at least talk with her? Maybe score a date?"

Sasha interrupts his interrogation with a forefinger in the air. "Or—a referral for a gastroenterologist?"

"No. No. And no. I was too busy trying to make it to the restroom before anything else came out."

Reliving what happened with Biggs and Sasha is almost as humiliating as the actual event. I'm a laughingstock. A meme. But not what the kids would call a "dank meme." Not a cute meme. Not a funny meme. Well, not funny to me, at least. The internet has crowned me the King of Memedom. More meme-worthy than any drunk celebrity at an awards show. More meme-worthy than a self-absorbed professional athlete who tells reporters at a press conference that he refuses to become a meme but becomes a meme because he pronounces the word "meme" as *meh-meh.*

The segment devolves in a play-by-play analysis of the puketastic affair. They rewind, replay, pause, and hit replay. They break it down frame by frame.

"Here's where it starts to exit his mouth!" shouts Sasha.

Biggs taps his smartphone and pinches his fingers out. "And here's the infamous Thousand Island fountain of failure!"

What I wouldn't give for someone, or something, to make that video and those memes disappear from the internet forever. An electromagnetic pulse would do the trick right about now. You know, an EMP. It could knock the internet off its kilter and erase everything. On second thought, no. Too extreme. I'd hate for us to get knocked back into the nineteenth century.

Oh, I got it. I could recruit that hacktivist group Anonymous to hijack the web long enough to scrub the video from the sketchy truck-stop bathroom of the internet. Wishful thinking.

Biggs throws up his arms and calls me "Ralphie McChuckface." He points to his watch. "So, did what happened over the weekend have anything to do with you having an immediate restraining-order-worthy crush on her? "

Before I can answer, Sasha interjects. "AC has a penchant for getting clingy at the sign of the smallest gesture." She clears her throat and swings her feet from on top. "So the city has to know."

It's none of the city's business. But I can't refuse to answer.

"It's true," I say.

"Ha!" shouts Sasha.

Biggs hits a button on the touchscreen monitor to his side. An air horn sounds. "Our man AC fell for a woman so hard, he threw up on her." Sasha announces it as a first in the history of radio contesting.

"Do we call Guinness World Records?" asks Biggs.

Sasha shakes her head. "We should get Bobbi's number from the promo department and set up a date. Just the four of us. And possibly Facebook Live.

"Fantastic idea," replies Biggs.

I swipe the hood off my head. Darting up and off the chair, I say, "Terrible idea."

Biggs nods his head in agreement. He gapes his mouth open and pokes a finger in and out a couple of times and continues, "You're right. Watching your awkward foibles with women is something I'm not willing to expose our listeners to on Facebook."

The embarrassment reaches a fever pitch until I realize that if I can score a date, then the humiliation would be worth it.

"I'm in," I say.

"Hold up y'all," Sasha demands, rubbing her eyes and leaning in toward her laptop. "We just got a text from..." She balls up her fists and plays a drum roll on the studio console.

Biggs's eyes widen. "Who?"

Sasha leans back in her chair and crosses her arms. Sasha's face beams. Her eyes sink into her sockets as she grins. "Things just got way more interesting."

"What do you mean, interesting?" I ask.

"We just got a message from someone named Bobbi Falstaff."

Uh-oh.

"Get outta here," says Biggs. "What does it say?"

AC is the greatest and I've decided to replace River with his name in my fan fiction stories is what I think.

"She wants to meet up for dinner."

CHAPTER 6

As I walk into Tencha's Tortas y Mas, the sizzle of fajita meat and scent of garlic and onions hit me in the face. At a rickety table, painted lime green and pink, right next to glass donkey with tequila bottles for ears, sit my dinner mates.

It'd be hard not to get hypnotized by her dimples, if it weren't for the Easter basket-like package of Pepto Bismol and IMMODIUM. Nestled in the stack of bottles and boxes of bowel-saving relief lies a plush toy, a stuffed intestine with wobbly eyes that spin around a clear plastic bubble. "Just in case—you know, well." Biggs hunches over with his arms hugging his stomach and inflates his cheeks. The others giggle, each one sipping from matching margarita glasses.

"Let's just say 'terms of agreement, '" declares Sasha, holding up a soggy napkin like it's some sort of business contract. I take a seat next to Bobbi. She and Lyla exchange glances and smiles. This is a good sign. Not a fake smile. Not where the risorius muscle pulls the outer lips down below the teeth. I know a thing or two from my dad. The night may end well. My internet pain, my gain. Hers, too.

Biggs dips a chip a bowl of queso, and plunges it into his mouth, dotting the table with orangish-yellow spots along the way. Sasha rolls her eyes at Biggs and breaks the silence. "Thank you for joining us."

Biggs grumbles something unintelligible with chunks of food sputtering out of his mouth. I've known him for several years, and his table manners have devolved since the day we met. He's like a drunk Viking at a conqueror's feast. With queso dripping down his chin, he slur-asks, "Why in the sam hell would you agree to hang out with this guy after what happened last weekend?" His tone suggests he's had a few shots. He wags a finger at me and grabs my shoulder. He's quite handsy. With specks of food shooting from out of his mouth in all directions, he clears his throat. This means Biggs is about to say something offensive.

I cut in. "At least this meeting has gotten off to a better start than the last one."

Bobbi snickers. "Ain't that the truth," she says, grabbing a chip and swirling it around in a bowl of green salsa. Turning to Biggs, she continues, "But since you asked, I did some digging and—"

The waitress swoops in front of her with a tray of food. A sampler platter of Tencha's finest, plumes of smoke billowing up from our bounty. "Excuse me."

I swerve to the left to peer into Bobbi's eyes from around the mound of beef, chicken, pork, and high sodium content. I lift an eyebrow and smile nervously. Bobbi returns the smile with one of her own. I grab a chip. I dip.

She lets out a sigh I thought would never end. "I did some AC recon on the internet."

She was getting to know me, as I was getting to know @muzikstan21. Beautiful.

"Because someone's internet presence tells the entire story of their life," I say.

Her lips purse together, then she smiles again. "What got me was the picture with that one-eyed dog."

The dog's name is Dolly. I met her at a pet expo at the Lecnac Grove Civic Center. She has one eye because her previous owner beat her half to death, and she lost an eye in the process. Her new parents nursed her back to health, and they take her to schools to teach kids about animal cruelty.

"Dolly is one of the greatest dogs I've ever met," I say.

"When he's not obsessing over people shitposting at him on Twitter, AC uses photo-ops with wounded animals to score dates," says Biggs. He holds up the number two with both hands and makes a hashtag, then says, "Hashtag facts."

I rub my fingers down my face, hoping the motion erases what Biggs just said. It doesn't work.

Lyla snickers. Sasha rams an elbow into Biggs's side.

"I could see love in your eyes," says Bobbi. She rests her chin on the palm of her hand and sighs. "And that's when I decided to reach out to your coworkers. Plus, I felt bad for all the crap you had to go through after—"

I interrupt. "The last thing I want is pity."

"The last thing Bobbi gives is pity," says Lyla.

"No more drinks for this one," says Bobbi, pointing at Lyla with her thumb.

Biggs, Sasha, and I glance over at Bobbi and Lyla, then at each other. They just want fodder for their next show. But they're on my team. I hope. You never really know in this jaded business.

It's what Bobbi and Lyla want that I don't know. In my head, I dance between "let's start over" and "let's ditch this place and never deal with these two again."

Bobbi clears her throat with a closed fist over her mouth to conceal its loud and growly nature. "What I should have said was, you seem like the kind of guy I'd like to hang around with."

A surge runs through my body from my stomach, up my arms, and into my head.

"But he threw up all over your shoes," says Sasha with a drunken slur.

"Don't sweat it," she says. "With my Nexus Radio winnings, I've got shoes for days. Scratch that, for weeks."

"Years!" exclaims Lyla, raising her margarita in the air.

Biggs holds up his margarita glass. His arm sways. He should have quit drinking several drinks ago. "I drink to that."

A quintet of jet-black-haired men approach our table, each one wearing a navy-blue mariachi suit with bullets along the sides and a bright red tie on their chests. "*Bom-bom-bom-BOMP-BOMP!*" shouts Biggs, Nexus Radio's resident mariachi connoisseur. We call him the whitest mariachi ever. Cade says his grito makes him more Mexican than me.

I lay down the only rule that applies when enjoying mariachi music at Tencha's: if you ain't hootin' and hollerin' by the end of their set, we can't be friends.

I pull out a $50 bill and hand it to the gentleman holding a trumpet with his other hand. The band continues. I recognize the song but haven't heard it in a while. Biggs starts playing the air accordion, tapping the fingers on his chest and extending his opposite arm into the air. He lets out a twenty-second scream. "Nice grito," I say.

Bobbi and Lyla light up. It's clear they've never seen mariachis before. Violins pierce the air with a song that triggers thoughts of my grandparents. Of seeing them dancing at family gatherings. Weddings, quinces, random family barbecues. And just like that, I imagine Bobbi and myself dancing in front of our families and friends. The deep sound of a woman's voice takes the restaurant hostage. Standing on a table is the band's lead vocalist. A twenty- or thirty-something with blonde hair, fair skin, and the most hazel of hazel eyes. The restaurant is a scene from one of those telenovellas my granny used to watch. "This song is what my parents and grandparents danced to at their weddings," I say.

Bobbi stares at the mariachis, bewildered by the singer's voice. She tries to recite the lyrics. "Voy, *ahhh...*"

"The lyric she's singing," I say, pointing at the singer.

"Boy...*ahh, booo-scar...*" She squints an eye and bites down on the corner of her mouth, trying to decipher the message.

I nod. "Un rinconsito in el cielo. It's about someone looking for a little corner in the sky for their love."

"I've never heard anything like this."

"I forgot how much I love this song," I say, watching one of the mariachi members slide his violin bow back and forth.

Bobbi wipes a pinky finger along the rim of her margarita glass, scooping up a dab of salt. She suckles on her finger and then takes a sip. Perhaps too big, as she squeezes an eye shut and rubs her temples. She shakes her head. Her hair flips to the side, sending a whiff of her perfume in my direction. She blinks and asks, "Why did you forget?"

The music has taken me back to my high school graduation party. The song blared through the speakers of our backyard. My grandparents, dancing cheek to cheek. Shuffling their feet across the patio floor of my parents' house. I had never seen them smile like that. "My grandparents are both dead. It brings back memories of a time that I'll never have a chance to revisit, I guess."

Sasha raises a glass. Her arm sways clumsily through the air like it's held down by a twenty-pound weight. "For AC's grandparents—salud!"

"Salud!" everyone shouts in unison.

Bobbi scoots toward me and places a hand on the back of my chair. From my vantage point, I can count her freckles. Something I can do all night. "The two of us can come back without these three and enjoy some music on our own," she says.

"Totally down for that," I reply, raising my glass for a toast. As soon as I raise my glass for a toast, a ping lights up my phone. It's the notification that I've been waiting for.

"Well, don't you look happy?" slur-asks Biggs, mouth breathing booze and beef torta into my face.

"Put your damn phone down and enjoy some actual human interaction," slur-shouts Sasha.

But I can't. There's unfinished business to tend to. I must finish what @muzikstan21 started. I feel like a sociopath, but it could be worse. I could be an actual sociopath. I just wanna have some fun at his expense, like he did with me. Like he does with others from behind his keyboard, that cowardly keyboard warrior.

Biggs pats my arm down. "Hey, what is it that you do for a living?"

Lyla cuts in. "She's River's favorite author."

Biggs's hand clamps down on the back of my neck. He bellows and breathes booze and beef torta into my face as he pulls me in. My face smears against bits of random tortilla chips and drops of stray queso. "Did you get that?" he asks. "She's...she's an ARTHUR!"

"Arthur?" yells Sasha. "I thought your name was "Bobbi."

Bobbi's face flushes pink as she bows her head down, looking at her near-empty margarita glass.

I tuck a cheek into the palm of my hand. After a loud, exaggerated clearing of my throat, I say, "She's one of the premier WattPad fan fiction authors, thank you very much." I turn and give her a wink.

Lyla clinks a fork to her beer bottle. Her eyebrows furrow inward toward the bridge of her nose. "True, but I'm still River's biggest fans."

"Only by a few pounds," quips Bobbi.

"*Ohhhhhh!*" screams Biggs, clapping his hands.

"I wanna know more about this fan fiction, though," says Sasha, swirling a tortilla chip through her bowl of salsa.

"Well," says Bobbi, slinking down in her chair. "It's just a hobby. Something I do for the heck of it. For now."

"She wants to go on a River bender and let him play her like his Fender," I say.

The mariachi music stops, and the restaurant falls into a strange two seconds of silence as I speak.

Bobbi, Lyla, Biggs, and Sasha answer me with parted lips and widened eyes.

I feel as though I confessed to a crime I wasn't aware of committing.

"Get the hell outta here, bro," says Biggs. "You read River Bronswell erotica?"

Bobbi buries her face into the palms of her hands. Then hoists it up and bellows.

"River Bronswell fan fiction," I say. Bumping a shoulder to Bobbi's, I continue, "Solid nine out of ten."

"Thank you," she replies.

Sasha snorts, launching a chunk of tortilla across the table. It lands by my hand. "Sorry," she says, drumming a hand on the table. "Next show, next show, next show…" But she's drunk, so all we hear is, "*Nehhhshow nehhhshow nehhhshow.*"

THEY CANCELED THE DJ

Biggs pounds a fist. I know where this is going, and I want to pound their future comments into oblivion. "AC, you're reading River Bronswell erotica—"

"Fan fiction," I interrupt.

He flaps a hand in the air and turns to Sasha and shakes a thumb toward my direction. "I can't wait to hear him read River Bronswell erotica on the air."

"*Yuuuuuus*," slurs Sasha, bellowing with her tongue swinging out of her mouth.

Because I haven't made enough of a fool out of myself in front of Lecnac Grove.

Bobbi exchanges grins with Lyla. Turning to me, she says, "Want me to pick the passage?"

I'd rather read a passage and swap my name with Rivers, actually. "Sure," I say.

Whatever gets me near her.

CHAPTER 7

E ngrossing myself in the wonders of River Bronswell fan fiction in the comfort of my own bed is one thing. Reading passages live on the radio, before an audience of half a million people, is a whole new level of awkward.

A River Bronswell poster drapes down the wall to the right of the mic in the control room. River goads me with a smirk. He points a finger outward so whoever looks at it feels as though he's addressing them. His smile teases me. Telling me to make him and his legions of fans proud.

Sasha kicks the door open, snapping me into attention. She tells me they narrowed it down to four passages, and Bobbi says I can choose one. Her curls bounce about her shoulders as she trudges to her side of the console. Slapping a binder on the counter, she locks eyes with me and smirks. "We even printed them out for you, my dear."

"How...kind of you."

"But you can get 'em," she replies. "I ain't your servant, and you already know I don't go into that hellhole of a copy room any more than I have to."

Biggs flings the door open. It bounces back and bumps his arm, splashing coffee onto him. "Shit," he growls. "Hey, we're on in two minutes and leading off with Mr. Fanfic."

Sasha tosses him a roll of paper towels from the cabinet next to the console and cranes her head back at me. "You heard our bearded bishop of broadcasting. Two minutes."

I spring up and head across the hall to grab my literary punishment from the copy room. A shell of what used to be a cool space—a tiny room where we used to store stacks of Radio Nexus merch. Shirts, iPad covers, iPhone covers, hoodies, games, and other stuff. Then came the Great Recession. And the layoffs and cutbacks. A time when midday hosts picked up web duties and night hosts inherited social media and receptionist duties. Now, it's a crowded room jumbled with useless crap nobody wants but is too lazy to take to the dumpster. A gumbo of life-size cutouts of "that one movie" from "that one guy" who ended up on some random E! show for D-list celebrities.

I trip over a crusty orange bin, scuffed around the edges, knocking it over and onto a stack of movie posters piled sky high. I stumble over a rollaway banner and bang my elbow on the wall. A wall that we used to be proud of because every artist who ever visited would sign it. The buzzing phone in the back pocket of my jeans hums against my ass as I slog through the cemetery of unwanted celebrity memorabilia. I fish it out and tap the face. A text from Bobbi. *Have fun reading my work this morning. I've got a whole bunch of readers tuning in just to listen.*

Leaning back against the wall, I shove the papers between my arm and my side and tap the phone with my thumbs. *Lol no pressure.*

The door to the studio flings open. "One minute," shouts Biggs.

Another message from Bobbi. *I wrote these passages just for the occasion.*

Which means she thought of me when she wrote these. Not River. Even though his name is gonna be all over the writing. But still, I am the reason she wrote this.

My texting fingers do what my mouth tends to do. Vomit words that shouldn't be expectorated. *Well, I'll be sure to replace my name with Riv-*

Biggs saves me from sending a potentially awkward text that would send me straight to the purgatory of unanswered texts. The fist of my insufficiently caffeinated colleague pounds the door. He mouths the words "hurry up."

I press the backspace button and hold it down, erasing the message. I reply with a smiley face emoji, shove my phone back in my jeans, and return to the studio.

"You ready?" asks Sasha. "Because I love me some juicy fan fiction."

"More like fan fuck-tion," says Biggs.

"He'll put the dick in diction," snarls Sasha.

"River's," whispers Biggs. He raises an arm. "On in three seconds." With his other arm, he taps the console three times, turning on each of our mics.

Biggs and Sasha open with their usual banter in the same way morning shows across America do. Weather, what they wasted their precious time watching on the idiot box. Then they transition their opening monologue into what they call a segment so steamy "we have to air it during hour one of the show, before the kids wake up." It's the saga of me and "the woman from Neat Feet Boutique." As the audience learns what I already know about Bobbi, the two sneer and make hand gestures at me. I reply with a fist of my own, shaking it back and forth in Biggs's direction and spreading my fingers to portray an explosion.

"AC, my man, you ready for your live reading of—" he shuffles the papers in front of him and clears his throat, "*When River Made Me Quiver?*"

"It won't be the most humiliating thing to happen to me this month," I reply. "This year, or ever." And nowhere near as humiliating as what I have planned for @muzikstan21.

Sasha pulls her mic down as she rests an elbow on the counter. "Bobbi—sorry," she makes air quotes with her fingers. "River's Favorite Author wrote these passages specifically for this occasion."

"I'm quivering already," says Biggs. An underestimated benefit of radio is that even though we can put video on the internet when we want, the actual broadcast is audio only. So nobody has to see Biggs circling his fingers around the nipples under his shirt.

Sasha continues, "And here's the kicker, if you can get through an entire passage without laughing or acting like a prude little bitch." She wiggles her nose and lifts her upper lip. "Then Bobbi will grant you a date because she knows that you take her work seriously."

Tall order, actually. These two will make it next to impossible to not laugh. What with their hand motions, body language, and facial expressions.

Plus, it's River Bronswell fan fiction. God, I hope my mother's not listening. Which means she is. Mother's intuition.

I pop open a bottle of water. Fidgeting with the bottle cap keeps me from focusing too much on the imminent embarrassment.

"Before we commence, AC," says Biggs. He raises a finger to tap the screen in front of him. "We have to set the mood." A tenor sax plays. Smooth jazz–type notes emanate.

"No, not that one," says Sasha, shaking her head.

A cheesy bass line starts playing. Upbeat with eighties-like synths. Something from an adult movie. So I've heard.

"That's the one," she says.

I can handle this. It's only fan fiction. Not some sort of box-of-tarantulas challenge. Fan fiction. Reading words. Words that'll go into the station archiver so they can put on the Nexus Podcast Page for the world to hear. So some River fan can share with another River fan. Who will share with another River fan, all of whom will tag River on Twitter and Instagram. They'll make TikTok reaction videos with green screens and fancy effects. But I can totally handle this.

"*Yezzzzirrrr!*" exclaims Biggs. "Showtime!"

The bass line plucks along. My mouth says nothing.

"Yo!" screams Sasha. Plucking her headphones off, she rolls her chair into mine. "He said showtime."

"Oh, right," I say.

The bass line continues. Biggs tosses a stack of papers into the air. A dove release of sheets flies up and crashes down. Like the slow torture of my life. "He can't do it!"

Sasha pulls the mic in front of me toward her face. Pulling me toward her, she says, "Oh ye of little faith. He most definitely can."

I swing the mic back in my direction.

"There's the AC we know," Sasha says, rolling back to her side of the control room.

"Atta boy," says Biggs. "Let's go, Lecnac Grove awaits.'"

Raising the paper in front of my face to block out Biggs's face, I begin. "Watching River caress the neck of his ukulele makes me long for his hands on my neck. His tattooed fingers, which, when balled into fists and held together create the sentence 'R + B 4 ever,' massage it."

"Yeah baby," says Sasha, biting the cord to her headphones. "*Grrrrr.*" Thankfully, it's Sasha and not Biggs saying it because I would have no doubt broken character.

"I long for those fingers to play my instrument. My body. I want them in my mouth. On my neck. On my back. Everywhere." And now I know my mom's listening because she always seems to be there when I'm not exactly at my best.

The air conditioner vent rumbles above, kicking in another cycle of wind. Which blows the paper down far enough to see Biggs flicking his tongue in and out of his mouth and rolling his eyes into the back of his head.

Don't laugh.

I clear my throat and adjust the paper to block him out.

"See this? River's voice echoes through the empty auditorium. He points to the center of what he calls his Ukemeister. 'You and I will make music more beautiful than anything that has ever come out of this sound hole.'"

Sasha snickers. "He said 'hole.'"

Don't laugh.

I continue, "He strokes the pristine piece of wood as he undresses me with his eyes, circling the sound hole with his digits."

A draft of air blows the sheet of paper down again, long enough to see Biggs waving a hand in front of his crotch and dry humping the air.

Don't laugh.

A date with Bobbi awaits. Just make it through this next passage. And instead of letting these two clowns ruin my flow—and my chances, I must lean into the situation. Tunnel fucking vision. I must...break into character. Shit, I hope my mom's not listening. "My lips quiver. I run a hand up my thigh, then along my arm, to warm up the chills that erected the hair on my arms. Those tiny tyrants commanding me to want him. To need him. To take him."

The music stops and a buzzer plays over the air. "That's it, that's it, that's it," says Biggs, waving his arms like a football referee. "You lasted longer than we thought you would." He falls over on the counter, laughing.

"I'm impressed," says Sasha.

"I'm a broadcast professional," I reply with a thumb in the air.

"I need a cold shower and something to cleanse the proverbial palate because you reading those words have ruined me," says Biggs.

"Now, about that date," I say.

Biggs and Sasha trade glances. "About that," says Biggs. "You were already gonna get one. We just wanted to embarrass you, that's all."

Awesome.

CHAPTER 8

I used to avoid Tencha's like a tourist avoids tap water in Mexico. Not because the menu was written in broken English to mimic the Chicano dialect. The chicken, I mean, *cheeeeeekin* tortas are superb. I avoided it because it became the hipster hellhole. A Mecca for handlebar-mustached manchildren who smell of patchouli and armpits. A haven for fedora-wearing misfits in Che Guevara T-shirts, sipping on the most cliché Mexican drink, eating some bastardized version of a torta.

But since Bobbi wants Tencha's, I want Tencha's. So here I am with the dimpled demigoddess, twirling her fingers through her hair. Staring at me mercilessly, she thumps my knuckles. "You ready to order?" she asks. She taps on her watch and clears her throat. "Not a ton of options here."

Bean and cheese. Carnitas. Beef. *Cheeeeeeekin.*

She's right. Not a lot to choose from, but I'm distracted. Not by her presence but by the presence of an old man in the photo behind her. An old man posing with a beautiful bride, smiling at me. Not the smile of a couple on the greatest day of their lives but the smile of a man who has intel on me. Beyond the baby-blue zoot suit with pinstripes and patent leather shoes. Beyond the pencil-thin mustache and thick, wavy hair combed back with the perfect side part, is a man who mocks me with a smile. He may have married the love of his life, as the picture suggests, but that man smiles because he's in my head. His grin exposes a dimple on his left cheek.

This man stands next to a beautiful brunette who's donning a large, poofy wedding gown, flanked by four toddlers. Two on each side, holding her gown. And the way the camera held their eyes, I get the feeling that they, too, know what I'm up to.

Bobbi waves a hand in my face. Her charm bracelet snaps me to attention. The smiley face emoji charm teases me. "*Yoo hoo*, dreamer boy."

A waiter approaches.

"Chicken--sorry." I stop and hold up a finger. "*Cheeeeekeeeen*. Two." I slam my menu shut and slap it down, adding a country twang to my voice. "Dos, amigo."

The waiter takes the menus. He forces an uncomfortable giggle and crinkles his nose. His face turns sour, like he sniffed expired sour cream.

Bobbi giggles. "Passive-aggressive much?"

"He's white, I'm not. So I can talk like their menu," I declare, tilting my head in apathy.

"Is the kitchen that interesting?" she asks.

"No."

"Well, I know of something that is."

I spoon a lump of gooey queso onto a chip, making sure to drop a jalapeño right in the middle. "Enlighten me."

"Have you checked Twitter?"

Taking a bite of my chip buys me a few seconds to avoid the question. I nod as I chew. "I try to abstain from that dumpster fire."

But I haven't abstained from that dumpster fire.

"Oh c'mon Aubrey," she says, lifting a beer bottle to her mouth. "It's only a dumpster fire if you choose to make it one."

"I like that you called me Aubrey and not AC."

She swills back a long sip of her brew, then points the bottle at me and sets it down. "Okay, Aubrey. Allow me to make you the—" She scoops up her phone and swipes at the screen. "The twenty-nine millionth person to know that River Bronswell heard you reading my book on the radio."

Shit.

"What do you mean, he heard me reading your book on the radio?"

The walls at Tencha's seem to close in as my stomach quakes. A repeat of the Neat Feet Boutique appears to be imminent as Bobbi tells me of the listener who recorded our bit and tweeted the audio to River Bronswell, who retweeted it with the comment, "Sounds like my kind of story. Might have to have this AC guy do a live reading when I'm in town lol."

The toucan piñata above our table mocks me. Its crooked, paper-mache teeth hem and haw. The laughing kids in the 1940s wedding picture on the wall facing my direction laugh at me.

"Wow," I say. "He tweeted that?"

Bobbi shoves her smartphone in my face. The light blinds me. I'd call it a good thing but not being able to see a tweet because your date keeps her phone too bright doesn't mean the words don't exist on the internet.

"You really think he'll come to town, and have you read my work in front of him?"

I hope not.

"Stranger things have happened," I say, taking a sip of beer, wishing it were a sip of the strongest tequila. Or vodka. "But it's a long shot. Someone as big as River Bronswell, even if he wanted," I continue, swirling the remaining contents of my drink. "Even if he stopped what he was doing and dictated to the world that he wants to come to Lecnac Grove for this," I gulp down the rest of my beer and shrug. "He couldn't."

Bobbi's shoulders slump. Then she sucks in her bottom lip and sighs. "Figured as much."

My phone buzzes. Cade. *Your performance was a hit with River Bronswell and his fans. Call me ASAP so we can talk about his visit.*

I turn my phone upside down and before I can catch myself, the words "fucking wonderful" escape my mouth.

"*Ruh-roh*," Bobbi says, clearing way for the waiter to serve her dinner.

"Nothing a four-dollar margarita pitcher can't fix," I say, lifting the drink menu and pointing my order to the waiter.

"Wanna talk about it?"

"Nah," I say. Scanning my eyes around the restaurant, I ask, "Ever see a photo of perfect strangers and feel like they know something about you? That, even though your lives are decades apart, they—"

"Know you."

"Yeah."

"Like they traveled to the future with you through some kind of—" She pauses to stare up at the ceiling and fixates her eyes on a chandelier made of empty tequila bottles.

"Simulation," I say before she can speak another word. It's a bad habit I can't shake, but she doesn't appear to mind.

"A simulation, yeah." She sips her margarita. "So, somebody here knows you."

I nod. "That couple on the green wall behind you, toward the top. The married couple."

"And what do they know?"

That the self-proclaimed Emperor of Pop Music will have me, his court-appointed jester, make a complete fool of myself on the internet because that hasn't already happened enough this past week and a half. And that I bought a jug of deer urine, printed a couple of @muzikstan21's less than stellar tweets onto a sheet of stock paper, laminated it, and dropped it into a giant glass jar. My take on Andres Serrano's *Piss Christ*, minus the Christ part because I'm not a completely garbage human being.

This newly married couple, the one with the mariachi group behind them —they know I disguised myself so I could stalk him for a couple of days. You'd be surprised how easy it is to find a cable company shirt at the thrift shop. This couple in the photo knows I bought a voice manipulator and recorded the worst fifteen seconds of @muzikstan21's life and sent it to his boss.

I take a chip from the molcajete-shaped chip bowl and dab it, making sure to scoop up a slivered jalapeño slice from the gooey pile of queso.

"Well," I hesitate and take a bite.

Bobbi gets playfully impatient with curiosity, pointing at her watchless wrist and tapping it with an index finger. "Well?"

This couple who celebrated their wedding night with dozens of family members and friends, they know everything. And the groom, with his sly grin, swagger, and charisma—this groom glares at me with equal parts approval and disapproval.

I take two more chips, making sure they're folded. It tricks me into thinking they're smaller. And smaller chips mean fewer calories. It buys me time. I cover my mouth with one hand and lift the other, suggesting Bobbi wait for me to finish chewing.

This zoot-suited groom knows I sent an important package to Plethora Plastics, Incorporated. An audio message for the ages. A message accompanied by a glass jar of animal liquids and a printout of a tweet. A message with my voice disguised as his. This is twenty-first-century America. Our gift is our curse. And that cursed gift is technology.

My gift to his boss is my enemy's cure. But sometimes you must be cursed to be cured. Bobbi glances at the photo behind her. "They do give off a time traveler vibe."

"They totally look like they were born in the 1800s and traveled to 1940 and are lurking around downtown Lecnac Grove as we speak," I say, taking a bite of my torta, encouraging her to talk.

"Kinda makes you wonder whether or not life is one continuous loop, and we never actually die," she says.

"Well," I swallow my chips and gulp. "There's no point in living if everyone lives forever."

"Oh, Aubrey," she replies, squinting her eyes. She slides her chair so it faces me and the married couple. "Everyone breathes. Everyone bleeds. But not everyone lives. And the ones who do..." She swivels toward me and sips her drink. "The ones who do live, they choose to do so, which means they never actually die. Like you."

"Me?"

I'm so consumed by my embarrassment that I've forgotten about my career.

"You," Bobbi replies, nodding in my direction. "Hey, you still haven't answered my other question yet."

"What question?"

I was hoping she forgot she asked.

"What does this gorgeous couple know about you?"

I flinch my left eye closed and purse my lips, pretending to examine them.

"*Ehh*...probably nothing," I say.

But I think they know everything. My phone rings. Cade.

"You might wanna answer that," she says.

"Nah."

No sooner than I reply does he send a text. *CALL ME ASAP*.

CHAPTER 9

C ade's voice echoes through the walkway leading to my apartment. "My text said for you to call me ASAP," he barks. The breaths blaring from my phone sound like they belong to someone who hasn't worked out in thirty years.

"I was down to fifteen percent on my phone and had to save the battery power for the Uber ride home," I say, hiding my white lie. "Barely made it home, bro."

"If there's something you wanna tell me, I suggest you do it sooner rather than later," Cade says.

His breaths are so distracting, I check the windows to see if he fogged them up from his house. I lower the smartphone, just in case his gusts of halitosis hit me through the screen.

"My date with Bobbi went well, in case you're wondering."

Silence meets me on the opposite end of the call, followed by a loud, overdramatic huff. "I don't care about your date."

"Something I said on the air?" I ask as I prod the key into the door to my place. I kick off my shoes, launching them into the wall, where they land next to my pile of running shoes, worn sneakers, and desert boots.

No answer.

"The woman who called my show to tell me about how she slipped in the lobby of an office building and everyone saw that she wasn't wearing panties. Did someone complain about that?"

"Surprisingly, no. Quit dodging me."

I turn on the TV to try and tune him out, hoping he gets the hint and lets me go. The news is on. Some five-person panel yelling at each other about the president. They're insufferable, but I'd rather listen to them than Cade.

"How can I dodge you when I have no idea of how, exactly, I'm supposedly dodging you?"

There's nothing on TV. C-SPAN. Yawn. Comedy Central. Some comic I've never heard of. Yawn. FX. Some weird reality show about tattoos. I'm not meant to binge-watch TV and ignore Cade.

Then he hits me with a proverbial punch in the throat. "You don't hunt."

"I don't."

"I went into your studio to borrow your headphones because I left mine at home."

"And that has what to do with—" I stop because I know the answer before I finish the question. He knows.

"What the hell do you need with Buck Love Magnet?" he asks.

I don't hunt and I don't even like the outdoors, save for my almost daily run. But that doesn't count. And Cade, a great outdoorsman, knows it. He knew from the first and last time he invited me on a camping trip. He and some of his neighbors took me. Chiggers and leeches attacked me like the Battle of Normandy. And my back was the shore. I broke out in hives. I got sick. My skin flared up for days. He never let it go. That he caught the biggest buck while I was hunched over in the tent. So of course he knew there was no need for Buck Love Magnet in my studio. Or my life. "I love the way it smells," I say dryly.

"Deer piss."

"Urine."

"*Urine* a shitload of trouble if you don't—"

"If I don't what?"

"Come clean," he fires back.

I remain quiet.

"AC, I know you and I know you're still going through some things because of all the extra attention you've received lately."

"And?" I growl.

"It's Lilian."

Ah, Lilian—the boss's boss and Nexus Radio's station manager. Nice, yet firm. Her zero-fuckery policy precedes her.

"Fine," I huff. "Sometimes you have to feed the trolls."

I continue to flip channels on TV. Rerun. Rerun. Basketball. Rerun. Rerun. Back to listening to Cade.

"You may not like it. You may not understand it or want to understand it, but you, my friend, are a high-profile radio personality. And you can't just go picking fights with random people on the internet."

He sets me off, even though he still has no idea why he found what he found or how far I plan to go with @muzikstan21. "First off, the internet picked a fight with me. And secondly, it's my obligation to set him straight."

"Set who straight?"

I flip channels, relaxing on my sofa with my feet plopped up on my junk-mail-riddled coffee table. Still nothing. Oh, wait. Some show about addictions. And a woman chewing paper. I'll keep it there. And change the subject to see if he notices. "So dinner with Bobbi was amazing."

"You went to that torta joint again. It can't possibly be amazing—and stop avoiding the subject. What are you doing? You've got deer piss pulled up at work. And I don't think I need to remind you that you're not supposed to—"

"Buy deer piss on company time with company property?"

"They say less than twenty-five percent of people tweet. So there's no point in letting one troll get in your head and stay there rent-free."

"Nobody's in my head. Sometimes trolls must be fed—so they can be starved of the desire to infest the proverbial waters of harmony in which the internet thrives," I reply.

If trolls are the poison of online activity, then I must infect myself with their poison. I'm the Mithridates of social media, infecting myself one troll encounter at a time. Slowly, carefully, and concisely administering the right amount, so as not to turn myself into a troll. Just one jar of Buck Love Magnet. Just one recording. Just one deep fake. Just one troll out of millions. A minuscule dosage. Just enough to make me immune.

Cade is one of the most high-strung individuals I know. He holds everyone to a high standard. We joke that when he gets to Heaven, he's going to make sure St. Peter is guarding the gates to the best of his ability. *A badge I wear with honor* is what he says. He raises his voice—something about there being over seven billion people in the world. He loves his numbers and facts.

I tune him out as I watch some woman shovel paper into her mouth. *How bad is the restaurant scene in her city, that she must resort to such a thing?*

The yammering voice on the opposite end continues. *Yadda yadda yadda*, "you're better than this."

Ugh.

Then he says that word. The word nobody wants to hear when their boss is lecturing them. The word that can all but assure trouble. A demerit, a strike, or worse, suspension. Or worse than that...termination.

I spring up, kicking over the stack of envelopes from my junk mail storage unit that nonslobs call a coffee table.

He hasn't stopped talking for at least a minute without breathing. He scolds me with the blistering anger of a middle school principal who caught a student skipping class. Something about how it's a shame to be so weak, I have to engage a stranger on Twitter.

"I'm not weak, bro."

Cade tells me to prove it. To tell him what I did or plan to do with the deer piss.

"I'd never use my status to intimida—"

"Sure about that?"

Dad always says that people who declare absolutes are the first ones to violate the terms of their self-righteous absolutes. Guilty as charged.

"*Fine*," I say, pacing around my apartment.

"Well?" commands Cade.

"All I did was laminate a compromising tweet from ten years ago, put it in a jar of Buck Love Magnet, and leave it with the receptionist where he works," I say, circling around the couch, navigating the terrain of envelopes and fliers in my living space, wishing that paper-munching muse on TV could magically appear and chomp away the clutter. "It was just the Muzikstan douche. Nobody else."

"Who are you?"

"Someone who's tired of being the internet's whipping boy."

"Stay off the internet and let's talk with Lilian Monday morning when you get in."

Before I can tell him that I don't do meetings with management, Cade hangs up. Lucky me.

CHAPTER 10

Bobbi scopes my digs, investigating the hall that leads from the door to the living room. She examines each picture in every frame—from the Independence Day montage with me and the Nexus crew, dressed in matching Uncle Sam outfits, to the Santa Bras fundraiser for breast cancer research. She squints her eyes, then widens them and smiles as she spots me. Her eyes shift from one frame to another, up and down with the focus of a boarding school instructor looking for the slightest speck of dust. I'd much rather a Saturday night apartment inspection from Bobbi than a Monday morning ass-chewing from Lilian and Cade.

"Well, this is cozy," she says.

"Thanks," I say, ushering Bobbi into my apartment. I find comfort in her approval. I spent a grueling fifteen minutes cleaning. Five minutes wiping down the kitchen with my last three Clorox wipes, five minutes rummaging through stacks of junk mail, and another five minutes dusting the living room and bookshelf with an old sock. Fifteen minutes more than I've spent cleaning all year.

"This is...interesting," she says, standing in front of my fireplace, looking at the painting above the mantle.

"I had it commissioned by a fan of the station. An independent artist who mainly does murals for corporations. But we're tight, so—"

"Are those beer cans and water bottles?"

"Gotta monitor my carbon footprint."

"Allergic to mediocrity," she says with a touch of sarcasm.

"The only allergy I have."

"I'll remember that, Mr. Cortes," she replies, taking off her sneakers and falling back on my couch.

I admire the piece above the artificial fireplace. "My dad always says the Cortes family has two allergies." Holding out a forefinger, I continue. "Laziness." Then I hold two fingers together. "And mediocrity."

"So I can expect an evening that's—"

"Far from mediocre, yes," I interrupt.

My phone interrupts me with a text from Cade. *Hope you're on your best behavior, Deer Piss Boi.*

My phone interrupts me with a text from Cade. *Hope you're on your best behavior, Deer Piss Boi.*

"Sorry, I need to reply. This won't take long," I say. "Make yourself comfy."

She obliges, sifting through the magazines under my coffee table. "Take your time."

I approach the bar that separates the kitchen from the living room and reply to Cade's text.

So you're my dad now. Cool.

Hitting send triggers an involuntary grumble.

"You alright?" she asks.

"Yeah."

"Ooh, *365 Ways Marcus Aurelius Can Change Your Life.*" She's in front of my bookshelf. And I forget for a second which books I slipped in my closet. Hopefully the ones about power and seduction. Can't have her thinking I'm a sociopath so early in the game.

"Kinda deep for a radio deejay," she says.

"Radio deejays can't rock with stoicism?"

"Just an observation," she quips.

"Observe away and see if you can make a decision about dinner while you're at it."

"Roger that," she says. "'Don't lament this and don't get agitated.' I like that one."

It's my least favorite of Marcus Aurelius's quotes at the moment as I read Cade's next text.

Behave yourself tonight, you're not responsible for feeding the trolls.

But I am. And if I could, I would feed them all. To each other. Let them eat and mutilate one another. It would make the world a better place. I bet Marcus, in all his infinite wisdom and mercy, would approve.

"I like this one," declares Bobbi. She clears her throat and makes her voice deep. "'How satisfying it is to dismiss and block out any upsetting of foreign impression, and immediately to have peace in all things.' I like this guy."

I don't want wisdom shoved into my head. If only I could light my smartphone and the Marcus Aurelius book on fire. It'd be my own version of *Fahrenheit 451*, minus the dystopian society. I just want a quiet Saturday night with Bobbi. And I want it without Cade and Marcus throwing a wet, moldy towel on the entire operation.

Another text from Cade.

You're not an internet archeologist. You can't just go back into someone's Twitter feed and dig for shit and ruin their life.

I can be whatever I want. So I am an internet archeologist. An excavator, pick-axing away at the dirt collected over someone's true persona. I am providing a service. I mean, I *was* providing a service to the internet before Cade lost his headphones and went through my studio. What I had planned was bigger than some science nerd finding dino bones and ancient Egyptian mummies. What I did for @muzikstan21 was worthy of *National Geographic*. Of the Smithsonian. Of the National Science Institute of Whacking Internet Trolls of America.

"You get what you deserve. Instead of being a decent person today, you chose instead to become one tomorrow," reads Bobbi.

If I didn't know any better, I'd suspect that Cade and Bobbi are in on this momentary portal into hell. I peel my eyes up from my phone to catch Bobbi's eyes hovering above the book. She lowers it and cocks her head to the side. "You seem...irritated."

I cross my arms, then lift a hand to fidget with the collar of my shirt.

"Well, dinner might clear your mind," she says.

"Yeah," I say, setting my phone down. "What would you like?"

Before she can answer, my phone beeps again. It's Cade. Again.

I got a message from one of the engineers.

I roll my eyes and growl.

She approaches the bar and scoops up her purse. Tugging it toward herself, she digs a hand inside and fishes out her keys, which are bound together by a cartoon image of River Bronswell. "I should leave."

"Terrible idea," I reply.

Her pillowy hand grabs my hand. Her flowery perfume hits my nose and makes me forget about Cade. For a split second. "You gonna answer that text?" she asks.

I don't want to, but I have to.

Cade's obviously been doing some digging. Some excavating of his own.

My phone beeps again.

He told me you were planning something with the RDS.

The good ole RDS, short for Radio Data System. The part of the radio that displays a station's frequency along with the title and artist of the songs they're playing. Sometimes they display ads and short messages like "Merry Christmas." Or in my case, *FOLLOW @MUZIKSTAN21 ON TWITTER TO SEE HIM GET WHAT HE DESERVES.* I only went into the workshop to ask a few questions. Perhaps I wasn't incognito enough.

"I rarely check in with my employees outside of office hours," says Bobbi. "Your boss seems a little needy."

Need I remind you that I once got fired for messing around with the RDS device?!?!?

True story. Three stations ago, Cade got so angry that a competing DJ called him out over a staged bit that he went into his employer's RDS and wrote a scathing accusation about him having an affair with his program director. Listeners believed the message. Lawyers got involved. Death threats were made. But at the end of the saga, Cade got fired, and he made industry headlines. Industry colleagues still talk about the incident.

"I'll answer him back," I reply. "Eventually."

She stands in front of the open refrigerator. "Typical bachelor fridge. Booze, old lunch meat, and a half-empty bottle of ketchup."

"*Fancy* ketchup, thank you very much."

"I've got a special fridge in the garage," I say to Bobbi, waiting to see if an idea of what to text Cade pops up into my head. "It's where the fresh meat stays. I get paranoid about cross contamination, so it gets its own space."

"*Awww*, are you suggesting you want to cook for me?"

Another text.

Answer me, AC. This is not a route any one of us wants to explore.

Bobbi hops on the kitchen counter, dangling her legs and swinging them back and forth, circling her feet. "I didn't know you were an Iron Chef."

I karate chop the air and scream, "Allez cuisine!"

"And the secret ingredient is...slaughtered cow."

Another text keeps me from cracking another joke at the expense of the Wagyu beef in the garage fridge.

ANSWER ME NOW.

I've never seen a smile like the one she's flashing. I've also never had such a polar opposite experience happen simultaneously. But we all wear multiple masks. Different masks for different occasions. A mask for strangers. Another for family. Another for the woman in my kitchen. Another for one of my close friends who also happens to be my boss. It's exhausting. Bobbi kicks a foot at me, hooking the back of my thigh and reeling me in. She cups my cheek in one and grabs my phone with the other. She sets my phone down on the counter beside her, leaning into me.

I catch a whiff of her hair. Honey and rosemary. She kisses me on the cheek, and it's a welcome surprise. She pulls my head next to her mouth. Her lips press softly against my earlobe. It shoots a chill throughout my body. This is the moment the awkward-looking fifteen-year-old version of me has been waiting for. And I'm frozen, a rigid mannequin. Her hands snake up and down my ticklish back. I nibble on the inside of my cheek to keep from laughing.

My phone beeps again. My apartment sounds like a video game. One that I know I'll lose. The stupid video game that costs two whole dollars to play but you know will end in less than two minutes because you're terrible at first-person shooter games. And after it ends in less than two minutes, you drop ten fucking dollars on the Zombie Terror World game because you're hellbent on killing something.

Bobbi lowers her hands and grabs mine. She pulls back and licks her lips. LL Cool J was the last person I saw lick their lips like that. I can't tell if she finds me attractive or if she wants to eat me. She bites the bottom of her lip, lowers her head, and whispers, "I've got nowhere else to be tonight. We can take as long as you want."

Cade could be firing me and I couldn't care less.

CHAPTER 11

M y parents are wrong about people who are friends with their coworkers and bosses. Americans spend more than half their waking hours at work. The least they can do for themselves is not spend those hours with a douchey despot crunching numbers from behind a PC running on Windows 94, atop a made-in-China, ergonomic throne bought on corporate discount from Office Depot. But as I walk into Cade's office, I now understand those corporate culture know-it-alls.

His feet are kicked up on his desk. Most 9-to-5ers could expect to see their supervisor dressed like an actual adult. But not Cade. Vintage basketball sneaks, ripped jeans, and a shirt with a picture of a cat dressed as an astronaut with meme lettering that reads, "CATALYST FOR SPACE TRAVEL."

It's hard to take this kind of manager seriously. It's hard to imagine someone who's vomited in your car seriously. It's hard to fear someone who's bought you Jell-O shots during a job interview at a bar. This must be why those employment experts don't encourage interoffice friendships.

"Cool shirt, bro," I say, grabbing a bottle of water from the bar in his office.

"Thanks for ignoring my text messages this weekend."

"Some things are better explained in person," I reply. I take a swig of water. Damn it, I'm not choking. I should take another swig and make myself choke. I can fall to the floor, break into convulsions, and Cade could call an ambulance. Then I could go to the hospital, and Cade could forget all about whatever he was going to talk to me about. The thought leaves my head. I don't want anyone to think Cade waterboarded me. "Besides, it was you who said that less than five percent of communication is verbal. Or was that some made-up crap?"

He avoids eye contact and spins his chair around to gaze out into the city's skyline. I wonder if anyone down on the street would catch me if I darted across the office and launched myself out the window. "You're right about that. But a simple 'let's talk Monday' would have helped."

"I was busy." Busy trying to not hurl all over Bobbi when we were making out at my place.

"With Bobbi?"

"Does it matter?"

He smiles. "Do you want to find out if it does?"

I raise my head high. "Is that a challenge?"

He stands up. "You dare challenge me with a challenge, young lad?" he asks with a fake Scottish accent.

I stand as well, shoving my chair behind me, playfully angry.

"From where doth thy burst of manliness arise, old *bruthuhh*?" I ask in a less convincing Scottish accent.

We slam our hands down. My palm burns. We move in on each other, locking eyes. We're fierce rivals in a duel. No, we're the friends we promised to be.

"Must thy constantly forget to brush thy teeth?" he asks, waving a hand in front of his face.

I stand back, self-conscious. I blow into a cupped hand and smell nothing. "Funny how your nostrils can't smell the bull crap emanating from your mouth."

"One of the greatest quandaries of the human experience," he replies.

I walk back toward his bar and pour myself a glass of whisky. "Since you're dying to know, yes, I was with Bobbi."

"Pour me a glass, too," he says. "And speaking of whisky, the engineers got pissed about your plan for the RDS. I had to walk them off the cliff."

Cade snatches the glass of whisky from my hand and takes a sip. He clears his throat and yammers on about how they want to tell Lilian everything. "I'm liable to end up with one of her stilettos up my ass because of you," he says.

He has me fix him another drink. And now it feels like I'm the manager and he's the out-of-control employee who's about to lose his job. "You sure you want another drink? It's only noon," I say.

He raises an eyebrow. He's the archetype of an angry boss. He grabs his cocktail glass and without a word, pushes it into my chest.

"Got it," I say. I never went to the principal's office when I was a kid, but I imagine this is what it was like. Minus the booze.

He paces around his desk, twiddling his thumbs in anticipation for his next drink. "Lilian has corporate coming to town for a report card on our station's performance. She told me the levels of fuckery must be held to zero."

"I hope she at least looked hot when she was angry," I say, trying to lighten the mood. I only say this because I know he's got a thing for silver-haired women in powerful positions.

Cade cages me in my chair. Circling me, he's a lion making sure I know he's the alpha. "Zero fuckery. And they want to have a meeting tomorrow, a breakfast meeting. So they're mad, but they're not 'mad mad,'" he says.

"But I didn't do anything with the RDS," I say, resisting the urge to raise my voice ten octaves and flail my arms around like a six-year-old who just pistol-whipped his little brother with a Nerf Blaster.

Cade sits on his desk in front of me. "Of course you didn't. But you went through some shit. And they're worried about you."

"It's not like I actually hurt the troll. I just wanted to get him back on course."

He shoves his glass into my chest again. I should hurl it across his office and show him who's in charge. But instead, I oblige.

As I continue to listen to the ramblings of a near-drunk best friend, it's clear to me that something's wrong. "Things worked out. Bobbi's interested in you. You should take the W and run with it. You don't ever see Hall of Fame QBs bitching about a botched pass interference noncall

THEY CANCELED THE DJ

from two seasons ago when they just won a championship," he says. "I wish I could just get inside your head."

"No, you don't. Trust me." Cade stands up and pats me on the shoulder. He kneels in front of me. It's weird. Now he's one of those "if you don't get help from Charter, please get help somewhere" dudes. He's the Michael Jordan meme. All he needs to do now is tell me, "Stop it. Get some help." I'm waiting for that one dramatic piano song to play, the one that plays during *Full House* when Uncle Jesse lectures the girls about something they fucked up. "You still need to work on your show, so let me cut to the chase."

I'm old enough to know that when someone with authority says, 'Let me cut to the chase,' something bad usually follows.

"I don't know what Lillian spoke with engineering about before calling me to her office. But she did mention the 'S-word.'"

"Suspension," I say. My body sags into a lumpy meat suit of misery.

"Let's hope for the best."

Sometimes being part of a severely understaffed team at a high-performance radio station run by a cheap corporation works in one's favor.

Cade gloats about his negotiation skills. *Blah blah blah*. He can talk Lilian into giving him foot rubs while wearing a whipped cream bikini. *Blah blah blah*. Then he goes dark. "But remember, my friend. No fuckery. Lilian's orders."

Got it.

He circles around me once again. His shoes shuffle and squeak across the wood floor. He drives home the obvious. "It doesn't matter how close we are." He slaps a half-drunken hand on my shoulder. The *thwap* echoes through the office. "She's the curtain caller. The boss. The one in charge. And she won't hesitate to fade your employment to black."

He pats my cheek. "Now get the hell outta here and have a kick-ass show."

"Knowing that I'm about to get shitcanned? Absolutely!" I shout, walking out of his office.

CHAPTER 12

I have many superpowers. None of them include flying around buildings, kicking bad guys in the balls with the bionic strength of a million gorillas, or sending them into another dimension. But nobody can match my ability to turn on the charm when Lilian emerges.

Her hair is the purest shade of silver, one hundred percent sterling. And wavy, like actual silver was melted into her pristine locks. And her eyes are the kind of green you see when you catch an overhead view of a baseball stadium, and you see the perfect green crosshatches. She's a modern-day corporate goddess. A true alpha female.

"Hi Lilian," I say, pretending to know nothing about her possible desire to send me to DJ Siberia.

She sizes me up. Her face, emotionless. Her posture, stiff. Her eyes fire Javelin missiles into my soul. Too bad I didn't vaporize. "Aubrey."

I only get called Aubrey at work when someone in management has it in for me. She sucks in, then releases her bottom lip and crosses her arms. "I don't have time to talk, but my guess is that Cade spoke to you about our offsite breakfast meeting."

Do you know that we all want to meet you for breakfast because we'll be bringing a box with all your shit in it so you don't have to come back to the station ever again? That's what I hear. My superhero power is putting words in people's mouths. "He sure did," I reply.

"Good." She turns her back and walks away.

"Lilian?"

She stops and turns her head to the side but her back still faces me. "No time, Aubrey," she replies. The words barely escape her nearly sealed lips. Lilian calling me Aubrey makes me more uncomfortable than the one time I caught Biggs and Sasha making out in the prize closet.

This is all one big misunderstanding is what I want to say.

The engineering department is overreacting again, and nothing happened is what I want to say.

"Are you sure you want to meet for breakfast?" I ask. "I'd hate to put you out of your way."

I see her shoulders move. A long sigh reverberates down the hall. Her back still faces me.

I'm convinced the halls will soon catch fire. And afterwards, Lilian will turn around to answer me. But instead of green eyes and an attractive face, it will be a monster. A monster with melted skin pulling down from her eyes. Singed eyebrows. A missing nose. A wide mouth, gaping open with ferocious fangs, dripping with blood and drool. Whiskers above her mouth. Peach-fuzzy hair collected under her chin. Her feet, instead of being covered by one of her expensive pairs of stilettos, are hooves. Her hands are claws. Claws with daggers for nails. Long, treacherous claws that could rip a heart out of its chest.

Lilian turns around and approaches me. The clicking of her stilettos echoes through the hallway, a clock ticking my life away. It's the longest ten-foot walk I've ever endured. Perhaps at the end, in one fell swoop, she'll remove one of her dagger-claws and stab me in the jugular and feed off the blood spurting out my neck.

She sighs again.

My superhero power is smiling a tone-deaf smile when smiling's the last thing I should do.

"You're the most adorable person who's ever been on my shit list."

"You need to put more people on your shit list," I reply.

"Breakfast. Tomorrow. And no fuckery until then or after."

Without giving me time to answer, she walks away. I turn around to head toward my office. Cade is waiting behind me, and he's in my face. "Tread lightly, my friend."

"Do I need to pack my things?"

He slaps my shoulder, the kind of consolatory slap that a head coach gives his star quarterback when they just threw a potentially game-losing interception returned for a touchdown. He wags a finger at me. I wanna bite it off, put it in my pocket, and feed it to the stray dog that loiters around my apartment building. "Don't ask me questions I don't have the answers to."

CHAPTER 13

Bobbi digs her hands into my shoulders. She's an artisan baker kneading the pasty dough that is my skin. Any harder and I'll end up with a puncture wound. I moan but make extra sure it's an "oh yeah baby keep going" moan and not the moan of a beta male with an affinity for Lifetime movies and lattes with extra whip, five pumps of vanilla using only fair-trade vanilla beans and cubed ice, not crushed. The thought of tomorrow's meeting has me wondering whether or not I should ask her to dislocate my shoulder with those powerful She-Ra hands. Then I could end up in the hospital and unable to attend.

A band of stray hair floats in front of her and tickles me. "So, how was work?" she asks with emphasis on "work," as she digs the heel of her palm into the part of my back below my shoulder blade. A touch more force, and her hand would end up through my back. Not good, seeing as how I haven't had much of a heart lately. My grumble is more of a reaction to her hands about to enter my body than her question.

"*Ermgh.*" She responds to my grumble with a grumble. "That bad, I guess."

She drops the subject, and we sit in silence for a moment. She adjusts herself so she sits cross-legged on my recliner. The light above creates a bright white dot on her thigh. I adjust myself so that I'm on a knee, in front of her. "I wish it were just 'bad,'" I say, making air quotes when I say "bad."

"Wanna talk about it?"

All I hear is, *Wanna talk about how you're so quick to set out and destroy someone's life because they trolled you on Twitter, and now you're about to get 86'd because you got caught?*

I place a hand on her leg. We hold each other's stare. My eyes make their way down to her River Bronswell T-shirt, The 2022 "Flow with the River" Tour.

Again, I refuse to engage her about my situation at work. My pettiness shall not get exposed. Not to her, at least.

It's already been exposed to management. But not to her. "I'd rather read excerpts from your WattPad story about River Bronswell in front of my parents and a roomful of priests," I say.

"I could arrange for that," she says with a grin that forces a dimple on her cheek.

"Don't you threaten me with a good time," I reply. "So what's for dinner? I can cook you whatever you want."

"Well, last time I saw your fridge, you had hardly anything in it. So sautéed ketchup, it is," she says.

I head toward the refrigerator. I open the door and clear my throat. "I went to the store and bought some *actual* food. Care to take a gander?"

Bobbi spins around so she's peering over the recliner. "Impressive."

"The choice is yours. Chicken or fish. Baked or fried."

"*Hmmm*, I'm long overdue for a cheat day. Let's go with fried."

Fried, like my career.

People who can decide what to eat in less than twenty-four hours rock. The "what do you want no you decide okay how about this anything but that okay how about this no not that" game gets tiresome. Plus, I kinda feel like something unhealthy.

"The messier the prep, the better the meal," I say.

"Alright, Chef," says Bobbi, bowing. "Let me know what you need me to do."

"Flour in there. Beat two eggs in this bowl, season with salt, pepper, Italian seasoning, and Tabasco sauce. And put the breadcrumbs in here," I say, grabbing a bowl from under the counter.

It's been years since I've made chicken tenders. My dad and I used to make them for Mom when she had a long day at work, typically on a Saturday night at the end of the month.

We ebb and flow so naturally through the kitchen, like Bobby Flay and Rachael Ray. Our movements are a flawless Viennese waltz on *Dancing with the Stars*. I glide out of her way. She slides between me and the counter. I wave my hand under the touchless sink for a splash of water. "Know how to tell when the oil's ready for the meat?"

Bobbi shrugs.

"Wet your hand and—" I flick a few drops into the cast-iron skillet. *Cshhhhzzzzz!* "Like that." Drying my hand on my shirt, I ask, "So, what's your end game with the WattPad thing?"

She leans a hand on the kitchen island and gazes upward. "Grandiosity, I suppose."

"I admire the honesty."

She describes an experience in high school with her English literature teacher. How he bemoaned her work as hopelessly shallow, destined for a one-way trip to the bargain bin of a big-box store. "So instead of letting his academic snobbery discourage me, I embraced it and channeled my anger into words on the screen. Hundreds of words turned into thousands. Which turned into hundreds of thousands of words read by hundreds of thousands of people around the world."

I could learn a thing or two about grit from her. "Sorry to interrupt," I say. "This is where we dip the chicken in the flour, then the egg...this is the glue that will get the crumbs to stick."

She crinkles her face and tells me she just got a manicure—but that she'll make an exception for today. I grab a pair of tongs from the drawer. It gives me a reason to rub against her. I make scissor motions with the tongs, snapping them toward her bottom.

We laugh.

"This is where Dad would tell me..." I lower my voice, "NO PLAYING IN THE KITCHEN."

We dredge, coat, fry, and return to her writing.

She talks about the difference between her and her high school English teacher. How she can inspire people to pick up a book after years without reading the written word, while academic asshats live in the squalor of their own snobbery. "I'm doing their job for them, and this isn't even my real job," she says, holding up air quotes as egg wash drizzles down her wrist.

"So," I say. "Why River?"

"Conventional wisdom in the literary world says, 'write what you like.'"

"And you definitely like River."

She raises her eyebrows up and down. "How many wipes are you gonna use on the counter?"

"As many as it takes to make sure my favorite guest doesn't get salmonella."

"I'm your only guest."

"My favorite guest." I clap the tongs together in her direction. "We'll boil this fresh pasta for a few minutes."

"Long enough for me to read you a passage from my new story."

"Only if you replace River's name with mine."

Her face flushes red. Before she can offer a response, I cut in. "So we take the pasta, place it in the skillet, pour the sauce. You layer the chicken and top it with the sliced mozzarella. And here you have it, chicken parm. The classic Cortes recipe."

Bobbi bumps her hip into mine as I play Tetris with the dishes in the dishwasher. She totally did it on purpose. A flash of hot rushes up my torso.

"So now will you tell me what happened at work?" she asks.

"You still haven't read me a passage from your new story."

"You can't avoid the question forever." she says, handing me a plate to load into the dishwasher.

I turn and look up at her. She stands over me. "I'd rather act it out." Her eyes devour mine. She grabs at my shirt and pulls me up. I stumble over myself and nearly fall back over the door to the dishwasher. The only thing missing is carnival music. We share a giggle, and she apologizes for nearly knocking me off my feet.

"No need to be sorry for showing me what you want," I say.

She grabs my head and leads it into her body. I'm face to face with the picture of River on her shirt. The look on his face tells says, "She'll have you throwing in the towel after twenty seconds, junior." That's messed up because based on previous performances, it'd be more like ten. She lifts the shirt over her head and tosses it to the ground.

What I need to do is actually what not to do: focus. On her, of course. On her and something not sexy, like old people. Old people with dentures making out. All that clicking and sloshing and their old geezer tongues licking each other's liver spots.

She yanks my shirt up and off. She claws at my other clothing. There goes that stupid picture of River on her shirt. Staring at me again from the floor. A wrinkled smile. *Eat a dick, River. I'm gonna think of you, and it'll*

96

help me last longer than ten seconds with Bobbi. Which is so much better than the ten seconds it'll take for Lilian to tell me I'm fired.

"We don't have to talk about work," she says.

"We definitely don't have to talk about your new story," I say.

CHAPTER 14

B-master's Café is everything that's wrong with dining in the twenty-first century. It's hard—no, impossible—to screw up breakfast. But add some fancy, highfalutin ingredients like imported truffle to a scrambled egg dish, and you have license to jack up the price by ten thousand dollars. Add "all natural, 100% organic, locally sourced and responsibly sustained" to your menu description, and you've got license to jack up the menu price by another ten thousand dollars. But foodies in Lecnac Grove don't care, and neither do the food bloggers— the ones who stand on seats, maneuvering the low-hanging light fixtures so they can churn out an Instaworthy post for their seventy-seven followers. Eat the damn food already. Something tells me Cade chose this spot just to annoy me.

#foodiechronicles

#nomnomnom

"What has caused you to become so cynical?" asks Lilian, over an auditory barrage of clinking silverware, plates, and shouting emanating from the kitchen.

I don't feel like I'm being judged. I know I'm being judged. Look at 'em. Lilian and Cade, sitting together like Judge Judy and Judge Alex. They had their judgy pants dry-cleaned for the occasion. Cade takes a swig of orange juice, his non-GMO, allergen-free, pesticide-free, seedless orange juice made with oranges imported from Heaven. "Listen, man. What you have to understand is that we could get sued, or worse, lose our FCC license over what you had planned."

"The FCC is nothing more than an unnecessary agency, an irrelevant elephant. Besides, they're not fining anyone because I never did anything," I reply.

My superpower is running my mouth when it shouldn't be running at all.

Cade, with a mouthful of scrambled eggs birthed by free-range chickens residing in a twenty-five-thousand-square-foot high rise in the city's east end, snarls. Lillian, with a mouthful of waffle bathed in syrup from Canadian maple trees massaged by half-naked male models, rolls her eyes.

I take a bite of my burrito, made with pork from pigs who bathed in a mixture of rare Himalayan dirt and unicorn sweat. It's...mediocre. Much like every other overpriced breakfast joint in this town. "Food's great," I say with sarcastic enthusiasm.

"It would be great if we could get you to simmer down and act normal," says Lilian.

I raise my hand like a second-grade booger who needs permission to speak in class. They eye-stab me. "Normal is ugly. Normal is repulsive. Normal is for losers. Normal is something I've never been and never will be."

Lilian dabs her face with a linen napkin made from the finest cotton, handspun by three-hundred-thousand-year-old cherubs in the Czech Republic. Just kidding. It was made by four-year-olds in a Third World country and sold at some wholesale place for a nickel. "We just need you to go back to what's normal for you."

She rants about "the problem with guys like you." How we all think we're above authority. That just because we bring in ratings success in a perpetually shrinking pool of talent, we think we're immune from discipline.

But I'm not one of those guys.

"So you brought me to this overpriced cafe to discipline me."

Lilian flashes a glance at Cade. His superpower is knowing when to keep his mouth shut. I wish I had that superhero power. "AC, you're in trouble, but you're not in 'trouble trouble.'" He makes air quotes when he says "trouble trouble." But when he makes air quotes, he doesn't bend his fingers. It's weird. He goes on and on about his first real radio gig. How when he was tasked with picking up a band from a nightclub and taking them back to the hotel, then to the airport. How, instead of watching them perform that night, he went back home to take a nap because he was tired. How he didn't hear his alarm, and his mom woke him up, yelling at him about someone on the phone, wondering where he was. And how the next day his boss told him, "Next time, there won't be a next time."

I gulp down my last sip of coffee, made with beans harvested by hands directly descended from Incan emperors. "So you're telling me there won't be a next time. Got it."

He and Lilian tell me to interpret the conversation any way I want. Breakfast with these two is like going into a confessional booth at church. Except they already know my sins.

They lay out my transgressions before me. The deer piss deep fake. The RDS message that I never even sent. A symphony of madness dances flawlessly between the clinks and clanks inside B-master's. Then they mention something about a visit from the corporate team.

My superpower is tuning people out when they say the word "corporate."

Maybe this overpriced burrito isn't as overrated as I think it is. It's helping me channel my attention elsewhere. They mention cutbacks. Typical corporate bull crap. Their modus operandi. Cut back until you're down to the VP running nights, answering phones, and posting to social media accounts in Bend, Oregon. Slash that budget until the CEO is pulling morning duties in Tacoma, San Bernardino, Denver, Kansas City, Dallas, Buffalo, and Miami, while answering phones in Los Angeles, Seattle, Salt Lake City, and Boise. Our market has been under a microscope, and we didn't know it until last week, I'm told.

Cade slumps in his chair. Not typical of someone who's always griping at me for my poor posture. His chin's raised high, and when he's not sipping on his green sewer-water-esque kale juice, he grins a punchable grin from ear to ear. Like he knows something. Lilian, too. "Last week, corporate pulled us into a conference call, AC."

Lilian stabs at her sack of waffles, doused with a Tony Montana–like pile of powdered sugar. "With upcoming cuts in underperforming markets comes a request from corporate." She raises the fork to her mouth, then lowers it to her plate. "They would like to make you its next syndicated host."

My parents would call this awesome.

You're being tasked with preserving and growing our brand on a national level, they say.

The art of weaving sonic satisfaction between songs is lost in this industry. And you will bring it back, they say.

Our industry continues to lose its uphill battle. But I'm the weapon that can help save it, or so they claim.

"At the expense of others?" I ask.

None of your concern, they say.

Creative destruction, they say.

I'm told that the company is not cutting off its nose to spite its face. I'm told the company is removing the original engine from a 1967 Mustang and putting in a new one. One that will help us win this battle.

"How could so much faith be put in me and why?" I ask.

"That you could ask such a question says everything we need to know. It shows that you're not just some run-of-the-mill, jock-in-a-box with an overinflated ego," says Lilian.

The waitress pours me another cup of coffee.

Cade hasn't taken his eyes off me. "I don't think we need to stress to you how big of a deal this is for you and for the company," he says.

More money. You want it, but to get it requires more time. More time requires more energy. More time, more energy, more money. I know how this plays out with the corporate promotion honeymoon phase. Then comes the eventual burnout. Then the high blood pressure and gray hair before the age of thirty.

I feel pigeonholed. "And if I don't want to be on the air across the country?"

"We all have choices," says Lilian as she spoons her coffee. Her telling me I have choices means that I don't actually have a choice.

She says we humans are a collection of the stories we tell ourselves and the decisions we make. I question her decision to bring me to a pretentiously overpriced breakfast joint so she can eat from a cup of bacteria and chastise me about my stories and decisions. Internally, of course. "History is his story. Your story. Is yours going to be defined by the failure to live up to your potential?"

My story. The one where I spend countless nights reading posts in Facebook groups and comment sections of radio industry websites reading comment after comment about another corporate giant replacing local DJs with some shill who probably kissed ass on his way to the top. I can see the posts and the replies already. *They replaced our afternoon guy of eleven years with some Vomit Bro who can't hold it together at an event. Shame!*

I bite my tongue because her tone has gone from excited to offering me a promotion to threatening my livelihood. My eyes home in on her stoic face, rosy pink with frustration as she turns to Cade. She leans in.

She's a lioness, closing in on the beta male of the pride. Not that I'm a beta male in real life. Well, not all the time.

Cade fidgets with the water glass in front of him. A lone bead of condensation drizzles down the side. He raises the glass and knocks back a cube of ice. "Take the promotion. Take the raise. Take this opportunity," he commands as he crunches. "And we'll forget about the deep fakes, deer piss, RDS messages, and anything else you may have planned for this @muzikfan37 person on Twitter."

"@muzikstan21," I reply without thinking.

"Whatever. What's it gonna be, AC?" Lilian asks.

I can't help but wonder if I'm being blackmailed. Swindled. Strong-armed.

But she's right. They're right. And I'm wrong. I could be failing to live up to my potential. All because of some social media pissant who doesn't know what I've been planning for him.

We eat our overpriced food in silence for a moment. Lilian's eyes remain fixed on me.

Cade's, too.

Suddenly, the overpriced burrito doesn't taste so bad. Suddenly, I realize that I got the girl. No, a woman. Bobbi. Forget how it happened and what happened in the following days. It happened. But that doesn't mean I should let some douchenozzle get me so wrecked that I throw away all that I worked so hard to get. And if I did, it would be an awkward conversation to have with Bobbi. "I threw up on your shoes the day we met, and the internet made fun of me so I acted like a bitch and lashed out and did some bad things and now my boss found out and I got fired. So, can we still date?"

I refuse to go out like that.

I dab the corner of my mouth with my napkin and take a deep breath. The inhalation sizzles like the sustainably raised bacon on the artisan-crafted grill in the kitchen. I exhale and take a sip of my brew. Lowering the mug, I clear my throat, just like I do when I'm about to do a break. "When do I start?"

CHAPTER 15

Since the turn of the century, fans have taken the meaning of "fanatic" to a whole new level. Gone are the days of a simple band shirt and tour poster. Those are for beginners. Artists who only go gold. And coffee mugs, tumblers, and smartphone cases? Those are for no-name SoundCloud artists who scored a two-hundred-dollar check in exchange for permission to use a clip of their song in a commercial for some dude's used car lot, starring the Used Car Lot Dude's daughter with that annoying kid lisp. Real fans showcase their diehard support with canvas paintings using blood and sculptures using the ashes of a dead loved one.

And nobody rocks the merch game stronger than River Bronswell, the highest-selling artist of all time. Shirts, hoodies, jackets? He's got the best designs. But those are for fake fans, the ones who can only name his radio hits. Any real River Bronswell fan has all the apparel, plus his complete line of talking dolls that sing and speak twenty different languages, including Aborigine. They have also bought his virtual reality games, augmented reality games, and vinyl dipped in twenty-four-karat gold, even though they have no idea what a record player is. They drink

River-brand vodka, tequila, and *River Tickler* whisky gets his fans drunk enough at shows to pay two hundred dollars for a limited edition, three-dimensional photo book.

Bobbi opens the door and ushers me into her townhome. She has everything. She waves a hand in the direction of framed magazine covers and articles featuring her home—in more languages than I can count. Fan art, created by her, lines an entire wall. Large pieces, small pieces. Art on canvas. Sketches in black and white. When guys show up to a love interest's home for the first time, they show up with a gift. Flowers, something. Anything. What I have seen in Bobbi's home makes me glad I have opted for something less tangible. It may cement my place in her heart.

Giant text covers an entire side of the hallway that leads to her apartment. It reads, "Mr. Bronswell makes my heart swell." The "Bronswell" and "heart" are red, the other words are black. The letters resemble what a serial killer would use in a note to a future victim.

"This is...interesting," I say with my mouth gaped open, pondering the fact that the authorities would consider her a person of interest if River ever turned up missing. For a split second, I consider rescinding my surprise. What she won't know won't hurt her. Or in this case, River.

Across the hall hangs a stained-glass image of River as a saint. Next to it, a Renaissance-inspired painting depicting River as a Roman emperor. I clear my throat and raise my chin, embracing the role of museum curator. "And here we have, the Marcus Aurelius of Pop Music, benevolent ruler of hearts across the Rivertopian Empire," I say with a horrible accent.

"Not much, but it makes me happy," says Bobbi, fluffing the River pillows and throw blankets on her couch. "Some might say I have an obsession."

"*Uhh*, slight obsession," says Lyla with a head nod in my direction.

A life-size River Bronswell statue stands in the corner. It wears a T-shirt with a picture of Bobbi wearing a River Bronswell T-shirt that reads, "I'm batty for River Matty." "Well, the obsession is only unhealthy if you have a River tattoo larger than the size of your hand," I say.

"Funny you say that," says Lyla. She turns her back to me and lifts her shirt up to her armpits. "I got this a few years ago, after Bobbi and I saw him in New York."

The tattoo is a ventriloquist doll version of River that was just told the operation didn't work, and he has three weeks to live. His signature locks resemble poorly drawn dreadlocks. The corners of his mouth are pulled down to his jaw. As if the tattoo artist felt sad for Lyla, so he created a sad River Bronswell.

"She got more than two hundred thousand likes on Instagram!" declares Bobbi, beaming with pride.

"And next up, Lyla shows me her collection of restraining orders," I say. I'm not joking. The tattoo screams "I collect jars of human eyeballs and wear leather belts bedazzled with noses and nipples."

"Behave yourself," replies Bobbi, pointing for me to sit next to Lyla. I oblige.

"I never thought I'd ever have a chance to sit on River Bronswell's face."

Lyla slaps my arm. "*Ewww.*"

Bobbi joins in. "Have some respect for the world's greatest musician and songwriter."

I lift my leg. "Fine, well, take comfort in knowing that I won't fart on him."

"Could I get you a bottle of Bronswell's Finest Brew?" asks Bobbi, walking to her kitchen.

Lyla raises her hand. "Yep!"

I turn my head to answer. "Jesus Christ!" Above the cabinets in her kitchen is a mural. It shows a teenage River Bronswell with long, wavy hair, dressed in a white robe, wearing brown sandals, sitting on a giant stone. In the mural, River is surrounded by a flock of sheep and several cows. Black V-shaped lines blanket the powdery blue sky. River is flanked by twelve men and a man in a white robe. The man next to River is beautiful, with a perfectly groomed beard, long hair, and a part in the middle. He sits with River atop the stone, his hands clasped and his eyes closed.

"Our Lord and Savior is River's biggest fan," exclaims Bobbi, snapping off a bottle top.

"True story," says Lyla.

If I wasn't as obsessed with Bobbi as much as she is with River, I would have left the moment I walked in. I wonder if she actually does have an army of cats hidden in a panic room filled with stacks of River fanfic books.

Bobbi pops open a third bottle. "Salud," I declare.

We clink drinks together.

"So what is this I hear about you being on the radio all over America?" asks Lyla.

"It's nothing, really. Just hosting a syndicated show in about—" I pause and glance up at the ceiling. A picture of baby River Bronswell holding up a bottle glances back. "About thirty cities. It's not that big of a deal, but thank you."

"Having a show in thirty different cities sounds like way more than nothing," replies Lyla, lifting her bottle and pointing it at me. "Congrats."

"He's so modest," says Bobbi. "But I'm proud of him."

I mouth "thank you" and kiss her cheek.

A Día de los Muertos–themed figure, about a foot tall, stares at me from the mantle above her fireplace, where she probably burns bad reviews of River's albums.

"So what's this I hear about you interviewing the Notorious R.M.B.?" asks Bobbi. She pulls out her smartphone from the pocket of her River Bronswell hoodie. *Tune in to Nexus Radio's AC to hear his backstage interview and exclusive announcement with River Bronswell before he rocks the Lecnac Grove Arena!*

"Funny you ask," I answer with the *boop* of my forefinger on her nose. Rubbing my hands together, I lean in to tell her about her gift. "This kind of stuff doesn't happen often, so I'm afraid this may be setting the bar a little high."

Bobbi and Lyla exchange glances. Their eyes widen. They turn and glare at me as I continue. They squeal as soon as I utter the words, "I'm taking you with me to the interview." And this must be what it's like when you give free crack to a crackhead. They heave themselves up from their seated positions and embrace, the same way Rocky Balboa and Apollo Creed did on the beach in *Rocky III*. As their hands slide across each other's backs, Lyla's shirt lifts up. The hideous River tat offers a menacing look. They spin. Lyla's initial smile has morphed into an emotionless expression.

'Bobbi pulls away from Lyla. She clasps her hands the way you would when saying a prayer. "Thank you, thank you, thank you..."

She interrupts her barrage of thank yous with a bunch of kisses on my cheek. Her soft, pillowy lips bounce up and down, and I want this moment to last forever. Until I see Lyla glowering her eyes and tightening her fists.

"You could give him a signed copy of your new fanfic," says Lyla under her breath.

"Unfortunately," I say. "Security is super tight at shows. Tighter than you'd think. Gifts from fans are forbidden."

That's a lie.

Cade expects to see a pic of River with one of Bobbi's books. Biggs suggested I read a passage in front of the two of them and film it for the Nexus social platforms. I told him to eat a big, fat one.

"I don't care about that right now, Mr. Cortes," she replies. I love the way she says "Mr. Cortes." It almost feels like we're about to act out a scene of one of her stories, with me playing the role of River Bronswell. A beardless, less musically inclined River Bronswell with about twenty fewer tattoos. "I'm curious—what's the surprise announcement?"

"I have no idea," I reply with my most Oscar-worthy attempt at skirting the question. River has a few days off after his upcoming show at the Lecnac Grove Arena. His people plan to use the city as a hub until it's time for the tour to resume. So Cade persuaded his peeps to commit to a Nexus Lounge performance two days after the show. But I only know that because Cade swore me to secrecy.

"Then we can be surprised together, I suppose," says Bobbi. And she mounts me, which is awesome except for Lyla's presence.

Lyla's head lowers and the blacks of her eyes lie below the thin lines of her furrowed eyebrows as her hands fidget and lips curl. She looks as though she's hatching plans to make us—or me—the subject of Netflix's *Making a Murderer*.

Bobbi runs her hands through my hair and down to sides of my arms. "What if you shared a passage from my new book with him? I could email you a couple and you can pick your favorite," she says. Her hands circle my shoulders. Then she squeezes.

I rear my head back and loop some stray strands of her curls around the back of her ear. "That would go about as well as me Googling pickup lines and reading them to Scarlett Johansson."

"Dost I detect jealousy?" asks Lyla in a fake British accent, snarling the corner of her mouth. She takes a River Bronswell pillow from the corner of the couch and squeezes it.

Bobbi scoffs. She dismounts me and falls onto her couch.

"That's more of a knock on—"

"Don't be self-deprecating for my sake, buster."

Buster. When a woman calls a grown-ass dude "buster," said grown-ass dude said or did something wrong.

Lyla rubs one of her forefingers on top of the other in my direction. "Shame."

"Really," says Bobbi with her head facing away from me. "I was just asking if it was possible to share with him something I made..."

I walk my fingers up her arm. She wiggles them away and stands up. Walking to the bookshelf, she grabs a River Bronswell nesting doll. She holds it out on her palm and wobbles it about. "It's not like I was planning to use my work as a way to propose marriage to him."

"You're right," I say. Even though your townhome suggests otherwise. "My response should have been more artful. It's just that these interviews," I adjust myself on the couch so I can look at her. "These interviews run so short. A ten-minute chat can blow by in what seems like thirty seconds."

Bobbi and Lyla grunt.

"Look," I say as I stand up. "If Cade called me right this second and said that instead of an interview, he wanted me to read your entire catalog of work in front of him, I would."

"Really?"

Not really, but I need an escape.

"Really."

And Bobbi leans over the back of the couch. She grabs a fist full of my shirt and yanks me toward her. "This is what I love about you."

CHAPTER 16

W hat people don't understand about backstage areas is this: they're uneventful, unsexy, and strangely quiet. Well, except for the occasion where you see a sound tech lose his mind over a malfunctioning wireless mic. "Where the hell are the double A batteries?" The stubby engineer with a mullet screaming at the top of his lungs at TD Garden in Boston is no different from the pit-stained roadie with a green mohawk and septum piercing throwing a tantrum at Humpin' Hanna's bar in Boise.

But back to the backstage area. To get into what every radio station bills as one of the most exclusive places in the world, you need to get to the loading dock. Once there, head to the security guard sitting outside the metal doors. Don't worry about the guard, though. He's harmless, despite the tough guy act. He'll check your credentials to make sure you belong, that you're legit. You know, to make sure you're not some terrorist or psychotic fan. To make sure you're a roadie—one who may be dripping with sweat who reeks of cigarette smoke and seven days without a bath. To make sure you belong backstage. And even if you don't belong, it's not like he could do anything about it. He's unarmed and about a hundred pounds overweight. Your ninety-one-year-old nana could take him out.

That's the kind of guard that greets me and Bobbi at the Lecnac Grove Arena. He points me and Bobbi down a drab hall, lined with unused trash cans, lighting, and sound equipment containers. Stacks of orange and yellow bins nicked with black and gray scuffs create a maze of oversized Rubik's Cube pieces.

When Nexus radio or any radio station gives you backstage access, this is what you actually get. Sell the sizzle, not the steak—never the steak. Indeed, if backstage experiences were steaks, they'd be the rubbery Salisbury steaks you had in third grade.

The good thing having about Bobbi with me is at least she knows what to expect next time. But hopefully there won't be a next time because hopefully she'll be so unimpressed by the experience that she'll never want to do or see anything backstage ever again.

"Congratulations and welcome to your backstage view of trash bins, storage crates, and a roadie's ass crack," I declare.

Bobbi's eyes don't blink. Her head rocks back and forth in awe. Maybe I'm jaded, spoiled, or both. What bores me and my industry colleagues is the Holy Grail for music fans. A Promised Land for rabid fandoms. To fandoms, their idols have traversed these hallowed halls and onto stages where they'd ingrain themselves into the culture forever.

The roadie with the tatted-up arms, dripping with sweat, ripped jeans, and calloused hands is just a roadie to me. A dude simply doing his job. But to fans, he may as well be a saint. Worthy of asking for an autograph. Worthy of a selfie that will be forgotten in a year. Worthy of a flashing in exchange for a glimpse of something other than an obscured view of sound and lighting equipment.

"Well, River's dressing room can't possibly be anything like this," says Bobbi. "I've seen pictures and videos."

"Of course not," I reply, escorting her to the waiting room. "But we still don't know if I'll interview him there or somewhere else."

I hope he invites us to his dressing room. Not because I'm nosy but because I already know what to expect if it happens there. Cade showed me his concert rider on the way to the arena.

Stories of his concert riders have leaked before. Animal-free products, ten dozen roses—pink and with all the thorns removed. A fruit tray consisting of only strawberries, blueberries, mangoes, and seedless blood oranges with the peel removed. Nothing major back then. That was TikTok River before signing his record deal.

Now our precious pop icon has gotten uppity.

Animal-free products now must be imported from Switzerland. Twenty-five dozen roses must now be pink, red, and black with no thorns. The fruit tray must contain fruit harvested at a farm no more than ten miles away from the Lecnac Grove city limits. Seventy-five bottles of water. Three bottles of top-shelf tequila and a dozen brand-new shot glasses. A coffee table with a mirror top. And finally, a razor blade.

My parents warned me about meeting my heroes. Your heroes will be the first ones to let you down, they once told me when I asked them to take me to a Comicon-type convention and they said no.

I never understood what that meant until my first few backstage experiences seeing fans fawning all over people who sing shallow lyrics for a living get blown off because they didn't look a certain way. Or because they didn't want to show their favorite band how far they'd be willing to go to demonstrate their loyalty.

I want Bobbi to meet River so that River will let Bobbi down. So that he can let the air out of her balloon of hope. Maybe she'll go from writing fanfic to a murder mystery about a musician getting disappeared by an angry fan.

I'm not cruel, I promise.

"This will be fun," I say to Bobbi. And now I can picture her at a bookstore, reading a passage about a murdered pop star. We walk down the hallway to a lounge area, complete with rundown tables, the kind with the connecting benches like we had in middle school. A couple of security guards wave us in. They point us to a table in front of an old, worn-out soda machine covered in dust. I should write with my finger "aspartame kills" the way a kid would write "clean me" on their parents' dirty minivan.

"'Sup," says one of the guards, a tall, stout individual. The kinda guy who's no doubt started his fair share of barroom brawls with the crack of a pool cue over someone's back. He bobs his head upward and smiles, revealing a couple of missing teeth up top. I can't help but stare. He senses me staring at the gaps in his piehole. Like it's my fault someone probably knocked them out for looking at his girlfriend the way he's looking at Bobbi.

Thankfully, I know it's always better to be authentically professional than authentic without a shred of professionalism.

"Just gotta wait here for River's people," I say to the guards.

The second guard, a short pudgy woman in her sixties, sizes us up. "You must be some radio star. Which one are you?"

The lesser one of 'em is what I think. A radio star in a faraway land because radio stars are not stars. Radio stars are the lowest in the hierarchy of stars. We're not even really stars. Remember that one little cousin who always tried to draw a star and it always came out looking like a deformed starfish? That's more of a star than me.

"Yeah, I guess you could call me that. I work for Nexus," I say.

"Ahh, yeah. That River dude was talking about your lady," says our tiny guardian of concert venues. She pauses and turns to Bobbi. Her eyes shift up and down, and her lips form a flat line of a grin and now she looks like the kind of person who's read all of Bobbi's work—three times —the first time alone, the second time at a book club, and the third time out loud to her pet opossum. She licks her lips and continues, "You're the one who writes about him, right?"

Bobbi and I turn to each other. She yelps, then covers her mouth with a hand as she presses the other on my back. Removing her hand from her face, she shouts, "Yes!"

Great. Maybe instead of an interview, River can read a passage of Bobbi's new book in front of me, and Cade can get another viral moment at my expense. My head droops down and a rush of warm shoots up my stomach and into the back of my throat.

Bobbi grabs my hand. "My favorite singer was literally reading my work."

This is literally not going the way I planned.

"He," I clear my throat. It burns from forcing bile back down the hatch. "He certainly is." I pat her shoulder and massage it.

She flinches. "I should ask him if my fanfic is the same thing as a DJ reading pickup lines to Scarlett Johansson."

The guards, the woman and her the toothless titan of a colleague, they giggle and walk off. They clearly want her to.

"I hope you do," I grumble and reach for my smartphone to check the time, even though I don't care what time it is because this night will last forever and that's forever too long.

"I think I will," she says in a way that sounds like that's the first thing she'll say when we meet him.

"Good," I say without making eye contact and I can feel her eyes locked in on me.

"Good," she whispers.

This ain't good.

CHAPTER 17

Bobbi does this thing when she's happy and sitting down. The bench squeaks on the floor as she circles her derriere. For a split second, I get jealous of the bench because of the way her hips wiggle about on top of it. But being jealous of an inanimate object is no way to go through life. And neither is obsessing over whether or not River and Bobbi will act out a scene from her book when I should be interviewing him instead.

Bobbi getting to meet River Bronswell is one of the most exciting things to happen all year. "Possibly ever," she says.

Like that one Christmas when she was a kid and got her pink princess bike with the pink and white tassels and purple squeaky horn. "Only better," she says.

Like her sixteenth birthday, when her parents had her going all year long about not getting a car. They told her they couldn't afford another car note and that it was either save for college or pay for a car that was only going to fuel her penchant for bad decisions. On the morning of her birthday, she woke up to see a beautiful red Mustang in the driveway. Today was like that, "Only better," she says.

Bobbi's happiness hypnotizes me long enough to forget about the visual of River reading her fanfic. She continues to wiggle her hips, humming some obscure River B-side. She stops and turns to me. "You don't ever get excited to meet anyone like this, do you?"

A question I get asked all the time.

"They all bleed red and breathe the same air as us. And they'll all eventually end up six feet underground. Just like you and me," I reply.

"A strange outlook to have," she says.

"Nothing strange about the truth," I say, gazing off into the doorway. A lone white streamer-like piece of paper blows between vents, trying to escape from its grasp. If that vent could talk, it could tell me what River said about Bobbi that had those two rent-a-cops so amused. But it can't talk. Like the universe, it's merely an indifferent observer.

"Well, I think it's pretty exciting that you get to interview him and that I get to tag along," she says, adjusting the sleeve of her blouse. "Even though I couldn't bring him an autographed copy of my book."

We sit in silence. The whistling of the vent and the buzzing of the soda machine are the only noises we hear. My phone vibrates. It's Cade. *Interview starts in five and River's people will be there in a couple of minutes.*

Bobbi pulls a compact and tube of lipstick from her purse. She pops open the mirror and slides the lipstick across her lips and smacks three times. Then she stuffs them back into her purse. "So what are you going to ask him?"

Certainly not his opinion of your literary musings.

"His thoughts on Middle East foreign policy and the advantages of switching to a gold-backed dollar, of course."

Her eyes disappear into the back of her head. "Seriously."

"Okay, okay," I reply. "Guess I'll just have to stick with geopolitical tensions between the United States and China and its effect on our allies in the region."

"Hardy. Har. Har," she says.

"The usual. His new album and the rigorous process by which he creates such compelling music every year."

Cliché questions to get warmed up. To wet the whistle, build rapport, and open him up. Every artist complains about getting asked the same questions. But deep down, cliché questions couldn't be more convenient. They're predictable and require little thought to answer. And when you're about to perform for thousands of fans on three hours of sleep, you need interviews that won't make you think too hard.

What's your favorite restaurant in [insert city name] here? How's it feel to be back in [insert nickname of city]? What's that one thing you have to do when you come to [insert name of city]?

A short, muscular guy with tatted arms walks into the lounge. The numbers 8-6-7-5-3-0-9 on his T-shirt stretch out over his chest. "Glad you're talking about the interview because there are some things we need to discuss before I take you back to the dressing room."

"Diggin' the shirt," I say.

"Child of the eighties, can't help it," he replies. He extends a hand. "I'm Skip, River's manager."

"I'm AC and this is Bobbi," I reply, shaking his hand.

"*Ahhh*, right," he replies with a smile that reveals coffee-stained teeth and two perfectly white ones on top. "Cade said you were bringing River's favorite author."

Bobbi rams an elbow into my side. "Did you hear that? I'm River's favorite author, just like my WattPad username."

"So about the interview," I say, ignoring her.

"Five to six minutes tops," says Skip.

Then begins the laundry list of do's and dont's.

No provocative questions. Nothing about River's appearance on *Thailand's Next Icon*. Nothing about his time at the now defunct Shut Up & Listen Records. Yawn.

I try to keep myself from tuning out Skip's list of commandments. Nothing too personal. Nothing about anything reported on TMZ or Perez Hilton. Nothing about the time he was caught on video peeing in a Grammy trophy.

I raise my arms in protest. "But that was amazing!"

Skip lets out a four-hour-long sigh. He crosses his gargantuan arms that could certainly squeeze my brain out of my ears with little effort. A clenched fist covers his mouth, and a vein worms its way up to the surface of his skin. His knuckles turn pink and white, then white and pink. "As I was saying," he barks behind clenched lips. He continues with his three-thousand-page list of demands, and I turn to Bobbi. I can't tell if she's bored or if she's daydreaming about River reading her work. "And nothing about his previous album."

The one that tanked because nobody wants to hear a ukulele over EDM beats.

My instinct to give listeners what they want kicks in. "But what if I framed it in a way that he could refer to it as a learning experience?"

"Nothing about his previous album," he repeats.

"Noted."

Skip squints his eyes. He pinches his chin with a forefinger and thumb, and I can't help but notice the pipe-sized vein twitching under the scorpion tattoo on his forearm. "River and our label's VP are willing to blacklist anyone from any of Sonic Fascination Records' artists who doesn't adhere to our guidelines," he says.

Bobbi's lips pucker and she begins whistling.

"Certainly, you don't wanna be the one that ruins our label's relationship with your parent company," he says with an air of condescension.

A risk I'd take if management didn't already have me on their radar. Too bad the interview had to happen after I got in trouble because I could be the fearless radio personality who defied a record label—for the sake of preventing River from talking about his girlfriend's books.

"I hate that we can't share a moment of vulnerability," I say. "For fans who could use a lesson in not letting one setback keep you out of the game."

Skip ignores me and ushers us down the hallway, toward River's dressing room. I swing an arm close enough to latch on to Bobbi's hand. Her grip is reluctant at best. Skip looks back at us. "So, *The Day River Played Me Like a Ukelele*, huh?

"Is it me—" She stops walking and fans the sides of her face. A pearl-sized bead of sweat drizzles down her cheek, creating a makeup-free scar on her face. "Is it me, or did it get unusually hot in here?" she asks. Her skin has turned school eraser pink.

"Definitely you," I say, convinced she'll hijack my interview to read him her smut while he feeds her grapes between paragraphs.

"Yeah," says Skip. The numbers on his T-shirt twitch as his laughter causes his pecs to bounce. "Definitely you."

We continue walking and the silence kills me. So I break it with the story of a kid who called the request line a couple of weeks ago. Skip's shocked that kids still call radio stations. "For River Bronswell, they do," I say. "So this kid, he thinks radio disc jockeys have all the artists on speed dial.

"I used to think that, too," says Bobbi.

Skip and I snicker. I start up again about this kid. This little runt who sounded no older than seven. He had a lisp, probably from a few missing baby teeth. I could hear this little booger rustling papers around. This kid's telling me how he can't wait to talk to River so he could ask him to go on a date with his big sister.

"*Awww*," says Bobbi.

"So what did you tell him?" Skip asks.

125

I make air quotes with my hands. "I gave him River's number. Eight, six, seven, five, three, oh—"

Bobbi interrupts and sings the last number. "*Nyyyyeeeeyiiiine!*"

The three of us share a quick laugh. Skip hums the ancient Tommy Tutone track, and I can't help but hear River singing a Bobbi version and using her phone number. He bobs his head about his shoulders, his hair fluffing through the air, and then he spins around. Pointing fake guns with flicking thumbs, he then knocks on a blue door that leads to Bobbi's Promised Land and says, "Showtime."

CHAPTER 18

Dozens of candles light up River's dressing room. Tall ones, fat ones, skinny ones. The smell of lavender reminds me of my visits to Lillian's office whenever I violate her zero-fuckery policy.

"River, we have visitors," says Skip.

River greets us with a nod. He's in some sort of zone. Some Zen moment. Maybe something to do with the mirror-top table he requested...or not. He flicks his fingers on his ukulele for a moment. Bobbi watches in awe, mesmerized by her favorite artist playing before her.

"You must be River's favorite author's boyfriend," says River. His eyes remain locked on the tuners of his ukulele.

I offer up an obligatory fake laugh at his aloofness. And for a split second I wanna swipe his instrument, swing for his head, jab Skip in the stomach with the handle, and leave Bobbi to survey the damage. Lucky for all of us, I don't act on the urge.

"I—"

"He is," Bobbi interrupts as she takes a seat on the couch across from him.

"I am," I say, glaring at River.

Skip slaps me on the shoulder, and it burns. "I'll leave the three of you alone," he says. He lowers his head so his eyes hover over his glasses and says, "Remember what we discussed. I'll be back in a few minutes." And he leaves the room.

River raises his head and locks eyes with Bobbi. Then me. Then back to Bobbi. And judging by the look on her face, she has the first half of a new fanfic mapped out. I think my bright idea has started to backfire.

"It's an honor to meet my favorite author," says River, standing up and grabbing her hand to kiss it.

"This is Bobbi," I say. "My girlfriend." He obviously needs the reminder.

"Nice to meet you," she says, scratching her neck, which has turned bright pink.

"What's it like to be the luckiest man alive?" he asks, extending his hand to shake mine. I want to grab it, squeeze it, pull him in, scoop him up, and body slam him through the table. But I don't.

"Amazing, actually," I reply, extending my hand to his.

The candlelit room provides low visibility. But I can see well enough to notice River's eyes glue themselves to her legs. The look on River's face is that of a douchebag who's about to swoop in and put the moves on her. And now it's clear that this will go better than me Googling pickup lines and reading them to Scarlett Johansson. Way better. For Bobbi, obviously.

Bobbi fidgets with her skirt and wisps her hair to the side. She's a shampoo model for a commercial that airs during a Hallmark movie, a movie about an overzealous musician and a radio personality's girlfriend. Except this one won't have a happy ending because the radio personality bludgeons the musician to death with his ukulele.

"I had no idea I had a favorite author with," he pauses and holds out his fingers, wiggling them one by one. "Seven-thousand, two-hundred ninety-six followers on something called WattPad."

Before Bobbi can seize the moment to tantalize River with her musings, I clear my throat. It breaks up whatever moment the two are sharing.

"Skip tells me we have about five to six minutes," I say. "So we can start as soon as you're ready, and we can be out of your way."

"What happened to your arm?" asks Bobbi, nodding her head toward the inside of his forearm. I wanna squeeze it so hard, a river of River's blood trickles down his arm and onto the floor.

"New tat," River replies, holding it up. He peels the tape-covered gauze back, revealing the words "Amor fati."

Love of fate. Nietzsche. My dad loves him and that quote.

"Love of fate, as in...?" says Bobbi.

River pats the couch, welcoming Bobbi to sit next to him. He doesn't acknowledge me, the one assigned to interview him.

"As in embracing everything that happens in your life," he says. "Good, bad, or indifferent. And seeing it for all its beauty."

As in not avoiding the inevitable, but embracing it. Even when that inevitability takes the form of a musician with no respect for boundaries with a woman he just met. In front of her boyfriend.

Under any other circumstance, I'd make a fist and yank it back and forth. You know, the international sign for jerking off. But I'm a broadcast professional, so I nod.

I clear my throat again. They look at me like I'm disrupting some pivotal conversation. Suddenly, I'm the annoying third wheel on a romantic date. "I'd love to talk about tattoos and Nietzsche during the interview," I say, plugging my mic into my phone.

"Yeah, sure," says River. "Whatevs. I'm down, bro."

"Mic check, one, two," I say, checking for sound on my mic.

River hasn't blinked once in the few minutes we've spent with him. He's licked his lips at least a dozen times. Something he's never done in the countless interviews and music videos I've seen. He asphyxiates her with fumes of toxic masculinity. Perhaps we'll make the ten o'clock news. I can see it now, some TV bro with Lego-perfect hair, a spray tan and a cheap suit breaking the news about a local area DJ whose girlfriend suffocated at the hands of a world-famous pop star. "Could your fandom put your life in jeopardy? Find out tonight!" Bobbi doesn't seem to mind the extra attention. I'm convinced this is the opening scene of her upcoming fanfic. And at this point, it'll be the opening scene of a movie starring Shailene Woodley and River Bronswell, playing the role he was born to play: an asshole. I see thought bubbles hovering around her head. "I should ditch AC for River" and "Bronswell makes my loins swell."

River asks us how long we've been dating. I'm focused on getting the mic right, so I wait for Bobbi to answer but all she has is an "*uhhhhhhhhh.*" To which I reply, "a couple of months."

Nice of her to remember.

———————

Five to six minutes with a global phenom like River is more like five to six seconds. His tour's going well.

Blah.

His fans are the best.

Blah.

He's so glad to be back in Lecnac Grove because Lecnac Grove fans know how to party.

Blah.

I should ask him about the mirror-top table. I should ask him if he thinks Bobbi's eyes are where her breasts are. But I'm a broadcast professional, so I don't.

"So let's talk about the new tattoo," I say, glancing over at Bobbi, who's staring a crater into River's soul. It's quite different from the mustached hot dog on your calf."

"It was a culmination of the death of my grandmother and the tanking of the last album," he says.

I remember the rules. But River's breaking them. Not me. This is my green light. "Care to elaborate?"

River goes into a diatribe about how the previous album was more of a learning experience than a failure. That he had to see for himself whether or not people would like his experiments. He talked about how his inner angst was the direct result of his inability to sell records and that he wished he sold more records with only one-star reviews than sell no albums at all. Because he would have the knowledge that at least the public felt something. But instead, the last album was a colossal waste of time because it kept him away from his grandmother.

His voice quaked with equal parts anger and sadness. "My grandma was the sweetest person I've ever known. Before I left to record that failure of an album, we spoke on FaceTime." He sat back, reached over for a tissue, and blew his nose. "She said—" He made this high-pitched, squealy old-lady voice, the kind you make when you imitate a grandmother. "'My dear, love your fate because the fate of your world lies in your hands. To not love it is to not love yourself.'"

Bobbi sits mannequin-like, frozen on the couch. She has enough material for at least two more stories.

I should ask him if he thinks his fans will buy this bullcrap. But I'm a broadcast professional, so I don't.

"How bad did it hurt? You know, getting the tattoo there, in that spot," I ask, pointing to the inside of arm. "Scale of one to ten."

He shrugs. "*Ehh*, I'd say about a four."

I should ask him if he'd like a moment alone with my girlfriend. But I'm a broadcast professional, so I don't. That, and I don't want to tempt either one of them.

Bobbi starts doing that shifty thing with her hips. I should ask how bad it would hurt if I hit him in the head with his ukulele or pressed one of these candles up to his private parts. But I'm a broadcast professional, so I don't.

"So what can we expect from tonight's show?" I ask.

River's eyes continue to motion up and down, waltzing all over Bobbi. Any other boyfriend would have said something by now. But not me. I'm a broadcast professional, not a brute.

I clear my throat. River probably thinks I have strep.

"Plenty of surprises," he says. "A couple of new songs, some previously unreleased material."

River stops and turns to me, then Bobbi. "And one lucky fan will join me on stage to sing a song with me."

Please pick me is the expression on Bobbi's face.

I'll pick you is the expression on River's face.

Get me the hell out of here is probably the expression on my face.

s Skip escorts us back to the break room where he met us, all I can think is how not awesome this is. He tells us to meet them by the left side of the stage, and now I wish I had knocked over the candles in River's dressing room and started a fire. Not a raging inferno. Just something big enough to make the authorities cancel the show. But here we are. And I see the writing on the wall.

"I can already see myself onstage with my favorite guy," declares Bobbi. Her eyes are glazed over, zombie-like.

"Strange how he's your favorite guy when you met him less than a half hour ago," I say.

Bobbi grabs my hand and swings it playfully. And without missing a beat, she says, "Well, my second favorite guy, next to you, of course."

"It looked as though you would have stripped his clothes off and straddled him on the spot."

Anger sweeps across her face. But instead of removing one of her heels and stabbing it into my eyes or taking off for his dressing room to strip his clothes off and straddle him, she lets go of my hand, almost throwing it down. "A little melodramatic, AC."

I reply with nothing because I feel like nothing.

Skip breaks the silence. "You two lovebirds work things out and make sure you're here at ten minutes before seven."

I grab a seat and pull it out for Bobbi. "I don't want to sit down," she mumbles.

"Oh, right. My gesture didn't include an invitation to sit on River's lap. My bad."

"What's with you?"

No way she's this clueless.

"You act like River's going to make a move on me tonight," she barks. We continue to sit in silence. The buzzes and flickers of the fluorescent lights above us flicker and buzz above. I home in on the sound. It gives me something to latch on to. Something to help me not say anything regrettable.

Bobbi paces back and forth. Her heels click on the floor. Clicking and clacking. More sounds to buffer the silence between us.

"I'd love to know what was going through your head back there," I say.

Bobbi's eyes sag downward, an admission of guilt. "I guess I was just starstruck."

"I could barely finish my interview because the ukulele Jesus was stealing you right in front of me."

The clicking and clacking stops. Bobbi turns and mutters, "I can't be stolen. Things get stolen. Jewelry gets stolen. Money gets stolen. Cars get stolen. I can never be stolen."

I think she thinks I'm judging her. And I am. Harshly.

She turns pink. But not like she was in River's dressing room. It's more of a reddish pink. She exhales short breaths out her nose. She wriggles her skirt, then circles her bangle bracelet around her wrist, desperate to avoid looking at me.

"Well," I say, extending a proverbial olive branch she doesn't deserve. "Do you think you can handle performing in front of about eighteen thousand screaming fans?"

She answers without a moment's hesitation with a resounding "yes" because of course she does, and why in the hell did I even ask? Because the experience will give her firsthand research necessary for at least five more stories. All of which will shoot to the top of WattPad's top ten most recommended fanfics.

We walk to the side of the stage. A sea of River fans appears all around us. Mostly women. Women in packs of three. Pairs of women. Women with husbands and boyfriends. Women with friends who think they're more than friends but will get tossed into the Friend Zone later tonight when their attempt at a kiss gets denied.

And the signs.

Someone quench my thirst for River.

River gets my juices flowing.

River can swim in my deep end.

And they say guys are boorish.

"Whatcha thinking about?" asks Bobbi.

How I botched the interview because of my amateur girlfriend is what I want to say. My plan for escaping this concert is what I want to say. Which song he'll open up with and whether or not it'll make you throw your panties at him is what I want to say.

But instead I tell her how awesome it is that she gets to join her idol on stage.

CHAPTER 20

T he stadium lights go dark, and the crowd noise reaches a fever pitch. Beams from a string of spotlights shine down on the stage, dancing side to side, then over fans in the pit in front of and around the stage.

Behold, St. River, the patron saint of getting women to throw undergarments on stage. The patron saint of hypnotizing women into a trance. The patron saint of getting women to involuntarily foam at the mouth at the sound of his voice.

"Make me your baby momma, River," shouts a fan.

Signs launch into the air.

"*Let me be your future ex-wife*," reads one.

"*I'd put my children on eBay in exchange for one night alone with River*," reads another.

"Willing to trade in my husband for ten locks of River's hair and a jar of his sweat," reads a sign right behind me.

St. River, the patron saint of snatching wives.

The spotlights turn blue, then red and pink. A bass guitar lick reverberates through the stadium.

"You seem quiet, compared to some of these other loons," I say as I nod my head in the direction of the pit.

Bobbi chuckles. "Just taking it in."

I know the answer but ask anyway, "So do you like River more, now that you've met him?"

"No."

I perk my head back and raise an eyebrow. And before I can say anything, she says, "I like him, way, way, *waaaaaaay* more."

There goes the bass guitar again. Then a kick drum. Colored lights along the side of the stage light up and blink. The sequence goes up and down as the fandom starts to lose its collective mind.

"Welcome to the Swim for Your Life Tour! I'm River Bronswell."

I didn't think the crowd could get any louder, but it does. My ears ring. Any louder and you'd think that Jesus Christ himself had walked out on stage.

River trots onto the stage and raises his ukulele. His black T-shirt with the letters "RB" in white on the chest. His jeans appear to be two sizes too small. He should have stuck with the gym shorts he wore back in the dressing room. But what do I care?

Bobbi's in awe.

"This first song is called 'One Tenth.'"

His voice is soothing, angelic. If I could nestle up to a voice and snuggle it, I would. He's that good. And his writing is better and about as authentic as it comes.

The lyrics of "One Tenth" move the fandom into an ocean of a thousand emotions. The three-and-a-half-minute autobiography that pays homage to his grandfather sweeps thousands off their feet. His grandfather, a Vietnam vet who performed surgeries in Saigon. His grandfather, a widower who raised his mother on his own after losing his wife to a random act of violence. The song's lyrics tell the tale of stars watching over them—how one is Grandma Louise, and the other is Momma. How one day, if God grants him the honor, he hopes to be one-tenth of the man his paw-paw is. The ukulele falls silent, and so does the crowd. Silence, minus a few random weeps. Some down low. Some in the back. Some in the cheap seats. Nose blowers, snot criers, ugly criers.

The seventy-five-foot jumbotron illuminates a huge, black-and-white version of River. He smiles. He wipes his face. He assures the crowed with a nod and looks down at his ukulele, then at the ceiling and down at the floor of the stage. He lifts his head and grins. Then he sings.

One hundred and ten percent, I will give
For as long as I live
to be the best that I can
to be one tenth of the man
but I will strive to be more
'til God shows me the door
to meet Momma and Maw
My sweet paw paw
So for you I give all
My sweet paw paw

to be one tenth of the man you are

I hope that's about as emotional as this set will get, especially since this is his first song. River's a smorgasbord of pop songs. His library boasts songs of college debauchery, childhood shenanigans, stupid decisions, epic parties, broken hearts, and disinterest in modern life.

"This next song, I wrote about an hour and a half ago. Hope you enjoy."

He fiddles with the neck of his ukulele. His fingers dance alongside it. Swooshes of air fill the stadium as he breathes into his headset mic. "The harmonies I came up with last night after a few adult beverages." River turns to the back of the stage. He lifts a hand up to his head, shaking it toward his mouth, indicating that he's ready for another shot. How he's not slurring his words is beyond me. In fact, how he's not passed out is beyond me.

A stage tech brings out another shot glass, then runs off stage.

His liver must hate him. He takes a swig of his drink. "*Ahhh*, I needed that," he declares.

The crowd erupts in laughter.

"On the count of three, let me know what you're drinking...one...two."

Drums roll a four-beat rhythm and a cymbal crashes.

"Three!"

Tens of thousands of answers fill the stadium. River turns to the side of the stage. He adjusts his hat and smiles at Bobbi, who hasn't blinked since he took the stage. "This next song is called 'Inebriated.'"

River strums his ukulele and walks toward the side of the stage. Our side of the stage. The spotlight follows. His breaths emanate throughout the arena with every step.

"But before we make this happen, I must invite the inspiration behind it."

I look at River, not knowing what I look like to him. He holds a hand out, motioning to me. "It's okay, bro. It's okay, it will only take three minutes."

I feel a hand on my shoulder. Bobbi's. "I don't know if I can stand," she says.

"Three minutes, c'mon!" shouts River, waving Bobbi to the stage.

Two security guards guide her up the stairs. Fans start to scream. "Lucky bitch!" shouts a voice from behind me.

Three minutes is all it takes. All it takes to send my life into another death spiral. Three minutes of Bobbi getting to hear the world's most popular musician tell her that she's the final piece to the puzzle of his life or some sappy shit like that.

My parents always say the universe gives you what you deserve. But I don't deserve to be constantly embarrassed on a global scale. A scale so global, I become meme-worthy fodder for a generation, a top ten trending topic of some infotainment TV magazine.

My face. I have lost feeling in my face. I'm humiliated but can't stop watching my girlfriend get stolen from me before my very eyes.

River lifts Bobbi's hand to his punchable mouth and kisses it. He backs away and strums a few random notes on his ukulele. He clears his throat and belts out his new song.

It's no exaggeration
No fabrication
My intoxication
Since the penetration
of your soul into my aura
which has shooketh my chakra

He stops, this arrogant asshat. He nods and winks. At me. As if everything's going to be okay. But I'm nowhere close to okay.

I should bum-rush the stage and rip his throat out with my bare hands. But I don't because I'm a professional. And I don't want to go to jail for persecuting the pop music messiah.

River turns back to Bobbi and rubs his eye with the sleeve of his T-shirt. He strums his ukulele once more and belts out the lyrics that will send me into oblivion.

Your presence alone could fuel the universe for infinity
but I want to hoard it for myself

He pulls the ukulele strap over his shoulder and sets it down. He grabs Bobbi, pulling her in for a hug. She embraces him back. He plants a kiss on her mouth. She returns the gesture by swallowing his tongue.

CHAPTER 21

I wanna pluck my eyes out, rub them into my shirt, and stuff them
back into my sockets because I don't believe what I'm seeing. A
group of fans behind me jeers. The group next to them cheers. I hear a
nearby glass drop to the floor, shattering into a bunch of pieces. A
metaphor for my life. Palpitations have my heart pounding into my chest
the way a drummer pounds a tympani.

My phone buzzes. A message from Biggs.: *Holy crap U aight?*

Then another message. This one's from Cade.: *DUDE WTF! Call me
asap!!!*

And one from Sasha:. *Want me to kill her for you lol*

I shove my phone into the pocket of my jeans and turn back to the
stage. Bobbi pulls herself away from River. I let out a sigh of relief. She
rears her head to the side, shifting her attention to the jumbo-sized
version of themselves on the screen behind River, then to the crowd. A
fan shouts, "Get it, girl!" as she pulls away from River. She turns to me,

shakes her head, and mouths "sorry." She wraps her hand around River's neck and plants another kiss on him.

The light-headedness wears off as I gaze into the jumbotron, that seventy-five-foot wrecking ball to my heart. Two perfectly pixelated tongues, prancing into one another's mouth. In Technicolor, then black and white and sepia. The swirling effects are a kaleidoscope of misery. The crowd roars in approval.

Awesome is what my mother would tell me. But this is not awesome. Nobody can make lemonade from the lemons life has lobbed at me. No chicken salad can be made with this steaming pile of chicken shit.

Then it hits me.

This *is* awesome. It's awesome because at least I wasn't brought on stage to be shot. Although that seems like a not-so-bad idea. What seems like a year of nonstop tonsil hockey plays out before me, and a dark feeling seizes and freezes me in my tracks.

Bobbi turns to me again with a broken smile.

"Lucky slut!" shouts a fan from behind.

As much as I want to shame that fan for slut-shaming my girlfriend, I can't. Bobbi's not my girlfriend anymore. Wait'll everyone finds out my girlfriend is with River Bronswell. My life is a reality show gone wrong. A reality show if you could turn a series of fail videos into memes. And memes into a reality show. I'm a living meme.

I turn to the jumbotron again. Her face glows, and I realize that River's right. She could fuel the universe for infinity. But I want nothing do with the universe. Not now, anyway.

River shifts his punchable face to me and tips his hat. "That was a life-changing song for me, and I thank you for sharing the moment," he says, turning back to the crowd. I raise my head to see where Bobbi went. The dark lighting, lifted stage, speakers, band members, security guards, and instruments impede my view.

I check my phone to see if Bobbi has sent me a text. Nothing.

This is every Dear John letter, every ghosting, and every bad breakup I and every guy has ever experienced. All at once.

I charge out of the stadium. My phone vibrates with more text notifications.

"Hey, you're that woman's boyfriend!" shouts a voice. I ignore her.

My trek up the stadium stairs continues. My phone in my back pocket vibrates again. I stop. It's Cade. I ignore.

"I saw you down there with that lady!" shouts another fan. I ignore her. I run up the stairs. Running from my fate. The opposite of amor fati. This is not love of fate. I hate my fate.

"You're that AC dude—you got ditched for River Bronswell!" shouts another fan.

"And now for another piece, a song I hope will inspire you to live life on your own terms," says River.

His ukulele fills the stadium.

"This is 'Go Get Yours.'"

He got his.

The crowd screams. A River fan steps in front of me. She's a tall one, slightly heavy set. Her homemade River T-shirt reads, *I "I would let River's river run inside me."*

"He got yours!" she yells as she points at me. Her friends and surrounding fans explode with laughter.

I maneuver around her as River starts singing.

You can't escape
No matter how hard you try
Life is sweeter than the sweetest grape
But the Grim Reaper's prepared to kiss you on the nape

I reach the top step. I pull out my phone. Twenty-three text messages. None from Bobbi.

Fifty-nine Instagram notifications.

The show will go on
Even after you're gone

Ninety-seven Facebook notifications.
So do your part
to make your mark

Laughter surrounds me. The voices of a few, but they're so much louder than the fans in the stadium.

Another notification. A text from Bobbi. *So sorry. I hope you'll understand one day.*

The world is yours
So damn it, go get yours

He got his. But he torpedoed my life in the process.

CHAPTER 22

The River Bronswell poster in the control room greets me with a toothless smile. Two black dots circled in over his teeth with black Sharpie. The word "asshole" is tattooed across his forehead in Old English lettering. And a crooked penis graces his cheek. Biggs's handiwork. But if he and Sasha were really on my team, they wouldn't have had Cade and Lilian strong-arm me into another appearance on their show.

Cade sits in the corner of the control room with his feet propped up on a file cabinet. His chin is raised and the corners of his mouth lower as he looks me over. "It will be amazing radio."

Amazing for Biggs and Sasha.

He ignores me again, and my gut tells me the best course of action would be to charge his desk, spin his computer around, see for myself who this keyboard warrior is, track them down, and teach them a lesson in Twitter etiquette. But I'm a broadcast professional. So I don't.

"Better than reality TV," says Biggs.

"Your life is a beautiful train wreck," says Sasha.

"Gee, thanks," I say, refusing to make eye contact with anyone in the room.

Let us lead the convo, they say. You'll be fine, they say.

"Easy for you to say," I huff, and now I wanna go into the engineering shop and douse it with a fire extinguisher and knock us off the air. That way, I don't have to air the dirty laundry of my love life on the air.

"Are you dead?"

Dead inside, yeah.

"Of course not," I answer, and too bad River isn't.

Delete your social media accounts, they say.

"I wanna delete River Bronswell from my show," I reply.

"Not possible and you know that," says Cade, enjoying the role of station tyrant a little too much.

"On in ten seconds," declares Biggs from behind the console.

Don't go off on River, I think to myself. Even though I want to.

"Whatever you do, go easy on River," says Cade with a hand on my shoulder.

"Nexus Radio with Biggs and Sasha and man, oh man, do we have a sitch," says Biggs.

This is the moment where I empty my entire vault of feelings into the airwaves of the most-listened-to radio station in America. Here, I can retaliate without fear of immediate retaliation. I can let Bobbi and River know what I think about their little stunt involving his shitty song.

"What in the actual hell happened to you last night, AC?" asks Biggs.

This is where I should show everyone that last night will make me, not break me. But I break down instead. Tears gush down my face, flooding the console in front of me. I muster enough willpower between sobs to utter the words, "My girlfriend left me for River Bronswell."

Sasha rolls her chair next to mine and wraps her arms around me. She smells of strawberries and basil, delicious. If I wasn't such an emotional wreck, I might hit on her. But then the image of her and Biggs swapping spit in the prize closet rids my head of any desire to do so.

"I'm not sure this has ever happened to anyone in radio," says Biggs. "You'll go down in the annals of history, right there with Marconi himself!"

With one arm clinging to my shoulder, Sasha grabs her mic with the other and yanks it toward her. "Hearing that he's the first radio personality to ever get dumped for River Bronswell before a crowd of thousands is something AC doesn't need to hear."

They speak as if I'm not in the studio with them, and I wish I wasn't. Snot trails out my left nostril and down to my top lip. I sniff it back into my nose.

Biggs and Sasha start a lightning round interrogation and it gives me no time to continue weeping on the air.

Did you hear from Bobbi yet?

What about River?

Did you know that the song he sang about Bobbi last night is trending worldwide?

Did you know that the label is releasing it to radio?

"No."

"No."

"No."

"He can thank me when he wins a Global Music Award for 'Song of the Year.'"

"Don't check the text screen," says Sasha.

I check the text screen. It's the most requested song because the fandom seems to relish in my misery.

The interrogation continues.

Did you know you're also trending worldwide?

Does this make you feel worse than the incident at the shoe store?

Would you talk to Bobbi?

What about River?

I'm glad my sadness can entertain people. My pain, their gain.

Infinitely worse.

Bobbi Falstaff and River Bronswell are dead to me.

Biggs smirks. "Awkward, seeing as how you play River about five to six times a day."

"Compartmentalization," I mumble.

Biggs takes a seat and kicks his legs up on the counter. "Oh yeah?" he says. "Enlighten us."

"We all compartmentalize, all the time, and we don't even know it," I say. "You take an Uber to the bar, not knowing the driver might hate your politics. You order food at a restaurant from a waiter who judges you for your cologne but never says anything about it to your face. Just like I'll do when I play River Bronswell and that godforsaken song during my show. Because I know what awaits him."

I say all these things between weeps and sobs. My superpower is making sense while sounding like a complete and total crybaby.

I turn to the pin board on the wall behind me. The schedule shows River's upcoming Nexus Lounge appearance. The one promised before the infamous concert. The name assigned to interview him is the last name I wanted to see but the first name I expected because the management team at Nexus Radio has a penchant for making my life miserable.

Cade's laugh besieges my eardrums as he gazes at his laptop. His eyes shift from left to right, up and down. Tiny crumbs of his breakfast shoot from his mouth. Bellow after bellow. Snort after snort. He's a twelve-year-old laughing at the bullies laughing at his buddy on the playground. "Someone check on @AConNexus. His girlfriend canceled him faster than his momma canceled their Christmas layaway when his daddy got fired."

And I wanna cancel this Twitter nobody with my fist to their face. But I'd settle for the @muzukstan21 treatment. Or a shovel to the back of the head. "What's their Twitter handle?" I ask, emotionless.

His head rears back. "Bro." His elbows smack down on his desk, and he rests his mouth against his clasped hands, sighing a stream of air into his fingers. He takes another bite of his taco. With a mouth full of masticated unborn chicken, he says, "These people are insane."

"What's their Twitter handle?" I repeat.

"Hold on," he says.

He ignores me again, and my gut tells me the best course of action would be to charge his desk, spin his computer around, see for myself who this keyboard warrior is, track them down, and teach them a listenesson in Twitter etiquette. But I'm a broadcast professional. So I don't.

"What's up?" he mumbles with a mouthful of food.

"The schedule," I mumble, "I saw a mistake on the schedule."

"Hold on." He takes another bite. He scarfs down the last of his taco with a bassy gulp and leans toward his computer. "@AConNexus, this HAS to be more painful than someone kidnapping you, tossing you in a van, and subjecting you to a recording of River's voice telling you your mommy hates you."

"It is," I say. And I can't help but wanna grab this Twitter twit, toss 'em in a van, and subject them to a recording of their dad saying their mom should have aborted them. But only a heathen would do such a thing. And I'm no heathen. "Now, about the schedule."

Cade chomps down his last bite, wipes a piece of food from the side of his lip, and flicks it away. He crumples up the aluminum wrapper and tosses it into his basketball hoop trashcan.

I launch myself up and swipe it away.

He snickers. "I'm not picking that up," he mumbles as he continues scanning his laptop.

"What...about...the schedule?" I get up to grab the piece of trash from the floor. "Dear Leader? Why did I see my name assigned to the Nexus Radio Lounge interview?"

"You're my boy," he says, and I hate it when he says I'm his boy. It always means one of two things. He's drunk, which he isn't at this moment. Or he's about to make me do something I'll temporarily hate him for—usually some bullcrap assignment that Biggs and Sasha got away with refusing to do because they're the morning show and everyone knows that they're the ones who *really* call the shots. Not him.

"And?"

Cade blathers on about how much Lecnac Grove loves the Nexus Radio Lounge, as if I didn't already know that. *Blah blah blah* three song set. *Blah blah blah* forty fans. *Blah blah blah* short interview.

"Okay." I wave my hands, trying to get him to make his point.

Blah blah blah Biggs will be out of town. *Blah blah blah* Sasha took the weekend off to spend with her parents—then he stops. His eyes sink.

The frown on his face looks like a melted photo, a distorted Snapchat filter. "There's nobody else to do it."

He turns his head, avoiding eye contact. And now I know the next thing he says will torpedo the rest of my day, and dammit, I just got into the office and my show doesn't start for another two hours.

"You're the only one," he says.

I'm the only one because Cade also doesn't do appearances. The station's lucky he records his show in advance. And nights? Nope. Syndicated.

"You should make Biggs and/or Sasha do it. They're the reason anyone listens to Nexus anyway, right?" I scoff. "Our listeners would be honored to breathe the same air as them."

Cade shuts his eyes, covers them with his hands, then grabs two fistfuls of hair. I'd love to pull it out for him. But I don't. His hands slide to his temples. He massages them. "It has to be you," he says.

"Fine."

"Thank you," he replies, relieved.

"I'll make sure to ask him if he and Bobbi have re-created any scenes from her fanfic," I snarl with a hand gesture to my mouth.

He presses his lips into a little slit. Blowing air out of his nose like an angry rhino, he paces around me. Stamping his feet extra hard, he yammers about the importance of treating the Nexus brand the way we would our mothers. And how our listeners expect us to rise to the occasion and stand above the fray. That *blah blah blah* Twitter is a microcosm of the people you'll ever experience and *blah blah blah* our listeners will be there for River, not the drama from the concert.

"It was a joke," I mumble, tugging down at my shirt. As if that adds any sort of toughness to my reply, which it doesn't.

"You sure?"

I didn't work overnights in Poughkeepsie fucking New York for two years followed by three years of evenings in Bend Me Over Oregon to let this break me. Sure, I'd rather spend a year's worth of paychecks on River merch and light it on fire in front of his fans than interview him in the Nexus Radio Lounge. But the former would land me in jail and make me unemployable. The latter would only test me.

"Don't worry," I say. "I got this."

CHAPTER 23

For once in my career, I'm thankful for the mundane tasks required of me during a live show. The counting of commercials. Reconciling the paper log to what's on the computer screen. It gives me something to focus on other than River and Bobbi hanging me out to dry.

I stare out the window of the Nexus studio and down upon the city. With no more forms to fill out and a four-and-a-half-minute song playing, I keep myself occupied by counting taillights.

This is when I would normally check social media and answer the request lines. When I'd razz listeners and let them razz me back.

I count up to twenty lights. Red ones. Slow moving. Fast moving. Trucks, cars, vans. A couple motorcycles. Some cop cars. Twenty-five lights.

This is when I *should* answer text messages or edit a phone call for my next break. But I don't because I can't. The red dots thirty stories below distract me from my task at hand. For a moment, I feel nothing. Just...emptiness.

My emptiness turns to envy. How I wish I could go where that minivan's going, barring the fact that it could be a mom on her way to pick up her dying son from a cancer unit. How I wish I could be in that sports car, as long as it's not driven by a thief who stole it and is about to get caught.

I walk away from the window, ready to change songs, envious of the police cruiser crossing the intersection below. The blinking red lights on the console remind me of the warning Cade issued—including a more imminent concern. A clause that management's adding to my contract. Our corporate overlords playing God once again. Cade told me I'm the only who can hold the line. Maintain order. And all I have to do is promise to not attack River during my show and on social media.

All I have to do is bend over and get screwed by my employer because management lacks the balls to defend me.

I slam a finger down on the button to fire off the next song. The first of a Nexus Radio Double Play, two songs in a row by the same artist. Song number one? "Loyal" by River Bronswell. If songs could be zip tied, covered with a hood, tossed into a black SUV with black tinted windowsing, thrown into a desert and set on fire. I'd do it to that song.

Funny how a word can trigger a memory: *Loyal*. Twitter beef. Twitter spat. Fanatical fandom. Rabid rabble-rousers. Then I get a digital itch that must be scratched. I open Twitter even though Biggs, Sasha, and Cade warned me not to. But I don't check any of my 248 notifications. I go straight to River Bronswell's profile.

His most recent post, time stamped 11:45 p.m. on the night of the concert, shows a collage of crowd shots and up-close shots of his performance. The caption: *Thankful for another great night. #Blessed.*

I check the replies. Then I check the counter on my song. Two minutes and forty-five seconds before my next break.

My next song is "Go Get Yours" by River Bronswell. Wonderful.

I scan through the fandom's replies. Part of me hopes for nothing mentioning me. Part of me is ready for someone to say something about me.

A bunch of "you're amazing" tweets. A few "Luv ya XOXOXO's." Some "flawless."

One minute, thirty seconds until my next break.

"We drove three hours to see you for my sister's birthday and we lost our voices. #WorthIt."

Then...

"You stole that DJ's gf hahahaha #epic."

"You started a war with that Nexus DJ and you gon' win daddy #RiverForLife."

That reply. That reply right there. Three hundred replies and one hundred retweets. One of them belonged to River himself.

I feel something come over me. It's hot. Then it's cold.

Thirty seconds until my next talk break.

I scoop up my headphones and slam them down on my head.

Twenty-one seconds.

Remember everything Cade told you, I think to myself.

Screw everything Cade told me.

Ten seconds. I turn the mic on. I clear my throat.

River wants a war.

Eight seconds.

He gets a war.

I slide up the volume to the mic. My eyes focus on the counter.

In a poetic moment in the history of my life, the final words to "Loyal" bleed out over the Nexus airwaves.

So do not soil your life
and all that you've toiled with words and deeds that can spoil
Be a good fighter and stay loyal

In that split second, I ponder the meaning of loyal. What it means to give and not receive loyalty. How being loyal means nothing in a world obsessed with everything but loyalty.

I turn to the schedule. The one with my name assigned to interview River in the Nexus Lounge. It makes me think of Lyla's plan and how it doesn't go far enough. It's missing a certain...something.

I lower the mic to my face and lean in. "AC on Nexus Radio and by now, you're familiar with the top trending story on the interwebs and in our city. And now, here's River with 'Go Get Yours.' You got yours, Mr. Bronswell. And for that, I salute you." Yeah, not really. I salute the ukulele I wanna set on fire and shove down your throat. But this will have to do for now.

CHAPTER 24

M om and I sit in silence on the patio of Tencha's. She holds the straw of her margarita to her mouth and smiles from behind it, a dimple appearing on each side. Cars whiz and whirl past us. The city hustles and bustles. We sip. We stare. We repeat. Horns blare. Tires screech. Pedestrians of all shapes and sizes walk past us as we watch from the patio. A pigeon lands on the wrought iron fence next to me. It moves like a robot, turning its neck back and forth, as if it's having a hard time deciding what to poop on. Or who to poop on.

"I hope it poops on me," I tell Mom. "I hear it's good luck in some cultures." I could use some good luck before my interview with River. And by good luck for me, I mean bad luck for him.

"Gross," she replies.

"But you can't argue with the fact that my life sucks right about now." And the only cure is seeing River drown in misery.

Mom sips her pink, slushy concoction and sighs the kind of sigh that indicates she's ready to unload a wealth of motherly wisdom.

"Life sucks if you let it suck the life out of you."

I hate talking with her as much as I love hating River.

"Do you want to waste another day thinking about this Bobbi person who you never bothered to introduce me to?"

I welcome the interrogation, begrudgingly. Like a good son does.

"Do you think they're wondering what you are doing?" she asks.

I should know the answers. Mom sits, staring at me, emotionless.

Yes, Mom. No, Mom. But I *do* wonder what they're doing.

"Stop, son."

"I can't."

"You won't."

"I can't help it, I thought that she was—"

Mom interrupts, nearly spitting a mouthful of Lecnac Grove's best margarita in my face. "The one," she sneers, bursting into laughter.

"You don't have to laugh about it."

She tears a piece of flour tortilla from inside the tortilla warmer, rolls a tiny dime-sized piece between her thumb and forefinger, and tosses it to the sidewalk for the pigeons. "You thought someone you met at a radio contest, whose feet you threw up on, was 'the one.' Sure, son. Whatever you say."

The pigeon swoops from the fences and down on the piece of tortilla. Then it flies away. "Maybe it flew off to go poop on someone who needs more luck than me," I say, looking upward at the pigeon as it shrinks into a tiny black speck in the sky.

"I was kinda hoping it would fly up and land a slimy turd on ya," Mom replies.

"So kind of you," I say, gently patting the top of her hand.

"I love you," she says.

"Love you, too."

We sit in silence once more. That's what I love about her and my dad. Sometimes just being with them, anywhere—even without saying a word—is enough to lift my spirits. We look at the birds flapping across bluest of blue skies. White clouds creep above and over the skyscrapers.

"Too bad we don't have a clear view," says Mom. She takes a quick bite of her fajita. A stray piece of shredded cheese falls from her mouth and lands on the table. "If we did, we could have one of our cloud picture contests like when you were little."

"Skyscrapers can't block my view of a giant spaceship flown by a white dragon ready to descend upon us mortals and take Bobbi and River away forever," I say.

"There's my boy," she says. Her smile makes me smile.

"So what are your plans for the rest of the day?" she asks.

Sitting on my couch, plotting River's downfall is what I want to say. I shrug, "Probably gonna go for a run. Might try for six miles. It's been a while since I've challenged myself to try a longer distance."

"Good, because you could use some sunlight, you're so pale." She takes another bite of her fajita, then starts barking orders with her mouth full. "Don't drink too much over the weekend. And stay away from women for a while. Find something other than chaos and debauchery to keep you occupied."

Easier said than done. I slurp up my last sip of margarita, circling the fluorescent green straw at the bottom of the salted glass, trying to get the absolute last drop to drip into my mouth.

"You haven't touched your food," says Mom.

"Not hungry, I'll save it for later."

A bus passes by, blowing dust and smoke into the area. A single piece of newspaper lands atop the bus in front of the patio's fence.

It's him.

"What's wrong?" asks Mom.

The headline reads, River Bronswell Donates Twenty Thousand Dollars to Local College, in Effort to Fund Music Program.

"Son."

"Mom."

"The most valuable piece of real estate you'll ever own is your mind. And now, this jackhole is living rent-free in it," she says.

"Hey, I didn't ask whoever threw that newspaper away to completely miss the trashcan, and I certainly didn't ask the bus to blow it next to us on the patio," I say.

"Your face is redder than my scarf."

"I thought I was pale," I reply.

She smacks the back of my hand with the back of hers. "Don't talk back to your mother."

"I was only reading Lecnac Grove's number-one newspaper," I say. "But enough about me, tell me about this veterinarian conference you're going to."

"Well, I was invited to deliver the keynote address, and I'm honored they chose me. But I'm an absolute wreck in front of crowds. A bumbling fool!"

"Oh, you'll do alright."

She stares off into the sky behind me and starts talking a mile a minute. Something she does when she's excited and nervous. "Easy for you—you talk for a living."

I look down at my empty margarita glass, wishing for more marg to help me keep up with my mom. She continues on about her speech to over two hundred colleagues from the American Veterinary Association. Me saying, "There's an association and a conference for everything" is enough of a comment to keep her going. Then a flawlessly crinkled piece of newspaper floats down and lies across the bush next to us. River's face graces the page, right below the headline.

"Will you talk about pet cloning?" I ask.

She describes pet cloning as a slippery slope, a Pandora's box. "What we start we won't be able to finish. Forget the ethical issues. What about the moral ones?"

All while River and I meet eye to eye. I smile and nod and agree and file my most pensive response as she continues her diatribe about cloning pets.

"They're not even the same animal," she says. She slams her fist on the table, causing the empty margarita glass next to my untouched, Instaworthy plate of food to topple over. "Sorry."

My default response is everyone's default response when a more articulate response isn't available. "I know, right!"

She continues, "Humans are so arrogant."

Especially River.

"We are."

"We think we can just manipulate everyone and everything so we get what we want without any fear of retribution."

"Tell me about it."

By now, the couple next to us has heard my mother. They watch in fascination, sipping their deliciously overpriced drinks. They foam at the mouth, waiting for mom to tell us how terrible this is for humanity.

"And Heaven forbid these tech companies don't try this with lions and tigers," I say.

"And bears," she replies.

"Oh my!" shouts the woman next to us.

Mom continues her diatribe about cloning pets while I continue to think about River. He's probably with Bobbi. In bed? Naked? In a shower? In a pool? In a jacuzzi? Naked? Will Bobbi be at the interview? Or will she take the coward's way out and stay back? All I see is River and his ukulele. In his Hawaiian shirt, riddled with pink and red roses and a lei. A lei that should be hung tight around his neck.

"I don't know, son," says Mom. "It doesn't seem to be worth fighting for. I might just play it safe."

The intrigued couple next to us shifts their attention back to their food.

"When has our family ever played anything safe?" I ask.

"You're right. I should throw down the gauntlet. I am one of the best vets in the country. Time to let them know where I stand. And my colleagues. Those too timid to speak up will rally behind me."

Just like those who've been screwed over by an ex will rally behind me when I show River who's boss. And as soon as I ponder how, a car pulls over next to the patio. Nexus Radio blares from speakers. I know this because a Biggs and Sasha promo plays. A short clip of their "Malevolent Mondays" bit from last week. "You put Ipecac in my jelly donut? You psycho—I thought I was gonna die!!!"

Mom snickers as the car drives off. "I heard that last week. He sorta deserved it."

River deserves it more. Then I feel my eyes light up.

"He did," I reply. And I laugh. I can't stop.

"Easy now, Mr. Schadenfreude," says Mom as she lifts her margarita for another sip.

"I bet he'll never steal people's lunches from the office fridge."

Mom shakes her head. "Who even thinks to use Ipecac?"

"A genius?" I laugh. A genius like that Nexus listener. And then it hits me. Me. A genius like me, using Ipecac. A lightning-fast highlight reel of River Bronswell interviews runs through my head and stops at my question from before the concert. The one about his donut tattoo. *Jelly donuts and women compete with one another to see which will be the death of me*, he said.

Spinning her fork through the refried beans on her plate, she continues, "Your dad hates that they still sell it."

"But he still keeps a bottle at home."

"He's a medical professional," she quips. Always ready to jump to his defense. "Besides, it's not like he ever uses it."

"When was the last time he bought some?"

Mom's eyebrows furrow. She leans back and crosses her arms. "Why?"

I shift my eyes to the sidewalk outside the patio. "Oh, I don't know..."

But I do. And now I know where to get it.

"Where is Dad, anyway?"

Mom rolls her eyes. "On the golf course, as usual. He asked me to go with him, but I prefer you to his friends who can't handle their liquor after the second hole."

I place a hand over my heart with my mouth agape. "*Awwww*." And I bat my eyes. "Well, since he's gonna be a while, let's ditch this place and go watch a movie. Your pick." *As long as it's something that'll keep you distracted long enough for me to snoop through Dad's stash.*

CHAPTER 25

W hen some radio stations boast about an all-access lounge, they're actually boasting about a conference room packed with twenty foldable chairs. All sizzle, no steak.

But not the Nexus Radio All-Access Lounge.

Legend has it, there was a Nexus newspaper called *Nexus Monthly*. It was designed and sold by one dude out of the corner of the Nexus facility. With the help of a few contributors, it became Lecnac Grove's version of *Rolling Stone*. But corporate gave it the ax during the pandemic.

The lowly corner office—once crammed with old computers, stacks of magazines, posters, printer paper, and ink cartridges—now plays host to musicians from all over the world. Solo artists, duos, and bands. Rappers with an entourage of twenty. Rockers with armpits that smell of rancid meat and patchouli. Former strippers turned one-hit wonders. Best-selling artists, artists trying to make a comeback after a stint in rehab. Instagram stars with followings of more than two million. SoundCloud stars just signed to a record deal.

And now, River Bronswell. The soon-to-be pop-music martyr.

Getting Dad's Ipecac was easy. Getting said Ipecac into River's body? Almost as easy. Cade doesn't believe me when I say I just wanna bury the hatchet and forget about the other night. He scans me and the boxes in my hands. "You're just gonna forget that River freakin' Bronswell kissed Bobbi onstage in front of thousands of fans and millions more on the internet?" He turns his back to me. Facing the stage, he continues. "After all of that, you're just gonna sit around, watch him perform the song he wrote about your ex-girlfriend, have donuts, and share a laugh?"'

"Yes," I reply with a smile. But not really. He'll never make it past his first song. His miserable carcass will worship the porcelain god the way his fandom worships him. It will be glorious.

Cade turns back to me. Twelve fifty-inch TV sets tower over him. They illuminate a dancing Nexus Radio logo, bouncing about from screen to screen. Every few seconds, the screens wipe left with an image of a Nexus artist. Then the screen freezes on a head shot of River, and I wanna hurl a chair at it. He lifts his chin. His eyes probe me. Then the boxes. "The other night, he said jelly donuts and women would—"

"I know what he said, I was there," I interrupt. Neither will be the death of him. Just his career. Next best thing. I raise the boxes up and tap the side with a forefinger. "Where do I put these?"

"Go ahead and leave them in the makeshift dressing room, that way none of our perpetually hangry interns get tempted."

"Roger that," I say. And I leave the Nexus Lounge. As I approach the makeshift dressing room, I think about my internet search for Ipecac stories. Teenagers using it to get sick at work so they could go to a party.

Bros using it to get out of going to their girlfriend's best friend's birthday party.

And the comments on Reddit.

I felt like death.

My stomach raged with the anger of ten thousand bulls.

I hesitate. How bad do I want to do this? Is his pain my gain? Will this make me feel any better? And what would my parents think? Yes, yes, yes. And—that doesn't matter right now.

A few paces ahead is the dressing room. Outside the door is River's entourage. Same as any other musician's entourage.

The laid-back engineer: outgoing but quiet, eager to talk about sound gear and chat about the Nexus setup.

The assistant: mostly assertive, sometimes bossy. Half the time female, half the time male. They're the gatekeeper. Don't look at the artist. Don't look at the artist. *You looked at the artist. I'm going to get my ass handed to me on the plane, you imbecile* is their vibe. The entire time.

The manager. In this case, Skip: a middle-aged dude. Half the time with a venti-sized cup of Starbucks. Mostly cool, but no time for jackassery. Some of the time with a lone earring, usually something dangly. Reminiscent of an 80s hair band.

The moment Skip and I lock eyes, he rushes into the dressing room. Probably to tell his darling little River that I didn't call in sick today. Then he steps back out.

"Skip," I say, pretending nothing out of the ordinary ever happened between any of us. I'm a broadcast professional, dammit. One prepared to set River straight.

"AC," he replies, fumbling with the collar to his button-down shirt. He's yet to make eye contact.

"I brought some goodies for the crew," I say, raising the boxes of donuts a few inches in his direction. "The top box," I pause to look down at it, "the top box is especially for River. I had my guy at the donut shop around the corner make these just for him."

"Well, we all know about women and jelly donuts," he replies.

I don't answer. Then I offer the boxes to Skip.

"Anything I need to know about the appearance?" I ask. "Just wanna make sure we're all on the same page with regard to time."

"Yeah, sure," he says. "He's got dinner plans in a couple of hours, so once we factor in pictures with fans after he performs," he bobs his head and mouths numbers as he looks up. "The restaurant's about an hour away, so I'm thinking about seven minutes before each song?"

"Okay, I'll stick with that timeline." Except I won't and neither will River.

"AC," Skip says as I try to scurry back to Cade's office.

I stop, but I don't turn to face him.

He says he knows how incredibly awkward this must be. How none of us want anything to go awry. That we should think about the fans. Give 'em what they want. A great interview and a killer performance.

"I know, my dude," I crane my head so I can see him in my peripheral. I hold a thumb up. "Great interview, killer performance." Except the donuts will kill his performance.

As I head to Cade's office in hopes of one of his world-famous pep talks, I spot the last person I want to see right now. The whole reason for the extra special donuts. I slide behind the opened door to get a peak. To see if Bobbi's there. Here. With him. Fidgeting with the tuners to his ukulele, sits River. His green trucker hat with a faded yellow smiley face covers his eyes. The lights shine down on the exposed knees of his stonewashed jeans. He leans into the mic in front of him. "Check, check. One. Two."

The microphone squawks with feedback.

"Sounds lovely," I shout.

River looks up. The ukulele pick in his mouth drops to the floor. Its click echoes through the studio. "AC?'"

"Welcome to the world-famous Nexus Radio Lounge," I say, inviting myself in, looking at everything in the studio but him. Scanning it for her. I turn to the left. Nothing. To the right. Bingo.

She wears a T-shirt like the one from the statue in her apartment. She slouches in her seat and pinches the bridge of her nose with a thumb and forefinger. "Oh hey, Bobbi," I say, matter-of-factly.

She lowers her head.

I ignore her ignoring me. "River," I say.

We lock eyes. I smile. His face remains blank. "AC."

"Well, I won't ask how you've enjoyed the past few nights in Lecnac Grove," I say, lifting my eyebrows at Bobbi. "So how about a story?"

"AC," Bobbi interrupts.

"It's really good," I say. "Promise."

I pull up a stool in front of the stage. River continues to fidget with his ukulele, and I wanna take it and ram it neck first into his neck.

"See that corner of the ceiling?" I ask.

He looks up as I begin the story of the Nexus Radio Lounge expansion. The story of what should have been a managed septic tank release that ended up being a busted pipe that spewed raw sewage and stench all over the floor.

By this time, the sound crew has gathered around.

They marvel at the permanent brownish-yellow oval that remains on the ceiling tile, entertained by the harrowing tale of the engineer and building contractors who had to go to the emergency room for a tetanus shot. They howl in laughter at the thought of having to work for days in an office that reeked of feces and cheap cologne because the assistant engineer thought it would be a genius idea to use cheap cologne instead of something antimicrobial.

River and Bobbi remain silent. Likely in disbelief that I have yet to bring up anything about the concert.

"Hilarious," says Skip as he waves River and Bobbi to exit the lounge and head back to the dressing room.

"Hilarious because you didn't have to work through it," I reply. But not the most hilarious thing that'll ever happen in the Nexus Radio Lounge.

CHAPTER 26

A few years back, Nexus Radio hosted some indie-pop band called the Banana Hammocks. Darby was out that week, so Cade left me in charge. Colossal mistake. We played Truth or Dare—but with a twist. If any of the band members refused, they had to eat a mystery snack. They landed on truth.

Truth: the rumor that you hooked up with your manager's ex-wife, who happens to be the record label VP's sister is the reason why the label dropped you.

They gladly ate the mystery snack.

Nobody told me was that the drummer was allergic to capsaicin, the chemical that makes spicy peppers spicy. In an effort to avoid drama, they created a life-threatening nightmare and gorged down their habanero-stuffed chocolate squares.

The drummer's face swelled up and he collapsed on his drum set. The laughs turned to screams as his body knocked over his drums. His drums knocked over his cymbals. Cymbals knocked over the mic stands.

Mic stands crashed to the floor. His body convulsed. His legs shook uncontrollably, banging against the cymbals. Lucky for the drummer, his bandmates gave him an epinephrine shot.

As listeners file into the Nexus Lounge, I wonder whether or not River already drank his Ipecac latte and whether or not he'll hurl during our interview or while he's performing. I hope for the latter—bonus points if it's during that stupid "Inebriated" song.

I greet our listeners, curious about whether or not they've picked a side. Mine or River's. Mine or Bobbi's. My hope is that they're completely out of the loop, in need of a cancellation of their subscription to *Behind the Times*. A quick search of River Bronswell's Lecnac Grove show pulls up a little more than ten thousand tweets and a few hundred Instagram posts. With my luck, every one of them knows what happened.

Listener after listener enters. A band director who plays in a nineties tribute band on the weekends. A grandmother and her grandson, whose mother died to the sound of River's music. And a brother bringing his older sister whose birthday is today—she'll never forget this day.

Skip and Cade give me the go-ahead to begin. And I can't stop laughing on the inside at the fact that the Ipecac is flowing through River's system, ready to purge him of all the wrong he's done to me. His fans won't like it. But sometimes we don't like the most important lessons life teaches us.

I grab my mic and tap the top with a finger. "Check, check," I say. "Welcome to another Nexus Live performance." One of the shortest performances ever.

Scanning the crowd, I continue. "Who got to see River's concert at Lecnac Grove Arena?"

Of the fifty in attendance, about half raise their hands and cheer. So half of these people saw what happened and have no problem with it. And now I hope the Ipecac keeps him in his dressing room and he never comes out.

"Alright," I reply, trying to maintain my composure. I clear my throat. "Well, Mr. Bronswell is definitely ready for all of you. And he told me before the performance that he'll be performing three songs for you tonight."

The fans hoot and holler. The women in the front, the two blondes with matching River Bronswell concert tees, they'll no doubt drown in River's bodily fluids. Fifty bucks says they'll brag about it on Twitter and refuse to wash their shirts for fear of bringing bad luck into their lives.

"And now, without further ado…" I look to the door. River stands next to Bobbi with an arm around her shoulder. His pasty face looks as though the Ipecac latte already kicked in. Good. Bobbi and Skip walk him to the stage and help him climb the four steps leading up to it. He holds the railing, hunched over like a sickly old man, as most of the fans mumble among themselves.

I rush through the intro. "Please welcome River Bronswell."

He places a hand on his stool, using it to guide himself down. Skip hands him his ukulele and it's unfortunate that he'll be hurling all over it.

River's head sways. Dots of sweat glisten on his forehead as the spotlights shine down on him. Too bad they can't incinerate his punchable face. "'Sup, bro."

I'm not your bro, bro, I think. And I see that Bobbi has taken a seat off to the side of the stage. She refuses to look at me, and I like it.

"Long night, last night?" I ask, knowing damn well I should have framed the question the other way. He'll say yes and brag about acting out scenes from Bobbi's fanfic. A perfect nightmare loop.

A handful of listeners giggle because they know what I mean and now I wanna serve *them* an Ipecac latte.

River removes his trucker hat and wipes his forehead sweat with his forearm. He fumbles with his ukulele and leans into the mic. His body sways, and it's too bad it doesn't fall off the stage. "More like, long afternoon." He smiles a broken smile. Ipecac will do that to ya.

"Well, we've got some fan-submitted questions and we'll get to that, but let's not waste any time," I say. "Let's begin with your first song in this exclusive Nexus Radio Lounge performance.

He nods. And his head swings from side to side. "This one's called, 'I'm an Ear.'" He begins singing the only song of his I like. His ukulele squawks a few missed notes and sounds as if a dying cat lives inside it. He sings.

If you need an ear
Do not fear,
For I am near, my dear

And before he can get to the last line of the hook, the part where his ukulele falls silent—the part where he's supposed to sing "to lend an ear"—he drops his instrument. A gulpy gargle reverberates through the lounge as he tries to maintain his balance by holding on to the mic stand. And it's beautiful.

River collapses and the crowd groans. He rolls over and onto his back. His head is a molten lava cake of puke. Bobbi's mouth is agape.

She'll never understand the irony of having two consecutive love interests vomiting in front of a crowd because of her.

"River," I say, bobbing about the front of the stage, trying to balance getting a good look at my handiwork with avoiding his fluids landing on me. He ignores me. and I hate being ignored. "Yoo hoo," River, I say with my head lowered, trying to make eye contact with him.

The screaming continues. Skip and Cade rush to the stage, then fall back as River rolls over and climbs up to one knee. He groans and mumbles, "Every time I say I'll neve—"

He falls to both knees again, and his hands lay flat on the stage. He straightens up and wipes his temples with the back of his hand. "Every time I say I'll never get wasted, I get wasted." And he hurls again.

Skip and Cade motion toward the door, waving their arms with the universal "come here" sign. Their request falls on deaf ears. Some listeners stand frozen. Others seize the viral moment in River Bronswell history. Let's see Bobbi put that in one of her stupid fan fiction stories.

Sour air clogs my nose. It travels through my nasal cavity and into my stomach. I take a deep breath through my mouth and say, "Please everyone, let's give River some privacy." *As much as I'd love for all of you to film it and post to all of your social media accounts.*

"Does this mean we don't get a picture with him?" asks a clueless fan. Adorable.

"Does it look like he's in any condition to snap selfies?" I reply.

River sits on his bottom. His head sags down as his arms rest on his knees. His shoulders twitch up and down. He moans a zombie-like moan.

Skip snatches the mic from my hand and declares, "Everyone out." He waves the mic in circles toward the door. "Please. Now."

As the remaining stragglers exit the Nexus Radio Lounge, one listener remains. A woman of about maybe thirty-years old. Tall and slender with super long arms. They're more like tentacles. She wears a plain white T-shirt under a River Bronswell denim jacket with a bedazzled River face on the back. This listener, she lurches toward River. In one fell swoop, she digs into the chest pocket of her jacket and flings out a phone. She calls for River. He looks up, coughing pathetic sounding coughs. More bile bails out on his body. The way I'd like for his fandom to bail out on him. And she snaps a selfie.

"Hey!" shouts Skip with his arms flailing about. "Enough!"

Cade darts toward her and escorts her out.

River collapses on his back. The sound of his head bouncing off the surface of the stage reverberates through the studio.

Remember when Lady Gaga went viral for vomiting at some barbecue joint during South by Southwest in Austin? Well, this is so much better than that.

CHAPTER 27

My alarm clock says 8 a.m., which means the humidity won't suck out what life is left in my body. So I stand and stretch. My hammies pull, teasing me. Trolling me. Tempting me to stay in and obsess over River and Bobbi.

I pull my running shorts up, shove my feet into the sneakers next to my bed, shake the sillies off, and leave. My feet pound the pavement. Just me, the whirring of oncoming traffic, and the birds. The pounding of my hangover and the lingering damage of a late-night fast-food stress-binge goad me into quitting. But Mom and Dad didn't raise a quitter. Okay, maybe they did because dammit my legs burn. And the tympani in my head won't stop drumming. And of course this has to happen right in front of the speed sign where Bobbi and I wrote our initials.

I clench my fist and pound the sign. As if that'll change anything. And I can already hear Cade, Biggs, Sasha, and Lilian. And every radio person in the history of the medium, including Marconi himself. "This is why you should never date a listener."

Blah blah blah.

"Oh shut up," I mumble to the imaginary voices in my head. Except for Lilian because she terrifies me.

I sprint toward the intersection outside my apartment complex. The walk light counts down from twenty seconds to one before I have to stop and do that run-in-place thing that only middle-aged dudes with bald crowns can pull off without looking like a dweeb. As I approach the curb, some prick in a Benz convertible screeches to a halt and tells me he's my number-one fan with his middle finger. Yeah, fuck you and the car you bought to make up for your shortcomings, I mouth but don't shout because I don't need any more conflict in my life. And he looks like the kind of guy who could squeeze my head into mush with his bare hands.

This is the longest three miles ever, and thank God I'm back. My legs sizzle as I dash into the elevator. The obnoxiously romantic couple next to me smells like cheap perfume and an impending breakup after a photo shoot in a field of bluebonnets. They can't get keep their hands off each other. Their fingers and hands and arms worm up and down their backs. The clearing of my throat is a nicer way of telling them to get a room. Then that godforsaken "Inebriated" song emanates from her smartphone, and I want to pull it out of her bag, slam it to the ground, and stomp a mud hole in it. But I don't. Because civilized people don't behave in such a manner.

The elevator dings, and I finally escape the presence of the couple who will no doubt wear matching jumpsuits to dinner tonight and brag about it on Instagram. And there, just as I turn the corner to trudge my exhausted ass into my place for a shower, stands the person least likely to be in front of my door. It's Lyla, leaning against the brick wall. She taps a finger on her wrist, then holds her hands up, preacher-like. Blowing a purple bubble, she struts toward me. Popping the bubble and smacking it in her mouth, she says, "'Bout time you came back. Bobbi said you ran slow, but wow."

"What do you want?"

My tone is not an invitation for pleasantries, but she responds with a smile. She stands between me and the door to my place. She takes a couple of steps back and turns to the side to watch her balance. Crossing her arms, she whispers, "I thought for sure you'd be happy to see a friendly face."

I wave her to the side and ram my key into the lock, pretending it's a knife in River's neck. "And I should be happy to see you because—"

Lyla swoops in front of me before I can open the door. Her perfume makes it hard for me to act like a complete jerk. My reflection in her sea-green eyes tells me she can see the same thing. A deflated buffoon.

"May I?" she asks.

She's all but let herself in.

"Sure," I reply, extending an arm to let her in.

As soon as we enter, she pushes me into the door. A hand presses against my chest and she obviously doesn't care that I'm sweating harder than a Nexus DJ in a room full of River Bronswell fans.

"What is this about?" I ask.

"You and me getting what we want."

I know what I don't want, and it has nothing to do with an intimate encounter with Lyla.

She backs away and invites herself into my living room. Circling around my living room, she homes in on my bookshelf. "One day, you'll date a fan of Bobbi Falstaff," she says. "And you'll be dragged to a theater to watch a movie based on one of her books. And that woman will yammer on and on about how the book is always better than the movie."

"And this has what to do with your presence?"

Before I can take a seat on my own couch, she holds out a palm and crinkles her nose. "Dude, don't get butt sweat on your furniture."

I grumble. She plops herself onto my couch.

"I'm waiting for you to tell me what you're doing here."

"Well, there's one way for that not to happen," she says, crouching to slide off her sneakers. Curling a leg under her rear, she leans an elbow on the arm rest and licks her lips. And if I didn't know any better, I'd think she's hitting on me.

I walk into the kitchen for a bottle of water and hold a second one up to offer her. She declines and hoists herself up. Her hands dig into her River Bronswell T-shirt. It stretches down and contorts his face. The way his face contorted as he blew chunks in the Nexus Lounge.

Mom says not to trust 90 percent of anything a woman pulls out of her shirt. Cash, a credit card that's likely maxed out, cigs, a blunt, whatever. Plus it's...gross.

She pulls out a pink piece of paper, folded into a triangle.

"I don't want that," I say.

She tells me to shut up. That if my mouth can kiss Bobbi, then my hands can certainly handle this piece of paper. That together, the two of us can get what we want.

"To be left alone by strangers on the internet?" I say.

No. Better.

She walks to the kitchen and grabs a seat on a barstool. Her legs dangle and swing in the air. I take the paper from her outstretched hand and lay it on the bar. After a quick pump of hand sanitizer, I rub my hands together and continue, "What is this and why on earth should I have any desire to know its contents?'" She says it could mean the end of River. Which means the end of River and Bobbi. Which means we both get the revenge we want.

I thought I was done with River after his Ipecac latte, but Lyla has me wanting to scratch another itch.

CHAPTER 28

I don't want to know how Lyla got this information. It feels illegal to even hold the piece of paper in my hand. Not to mention it was marinating in her bra on a warm spring afternoon. The edges of some of the lettering on the creased paper have started to smudge. Could be the sanitizer, could be her sweat. I hope it's the former and not the latter.

She says a good IT gal always gets what she wants. And she raises her well-trimmed eyebrows.

"How do you know I'm angry and want to use this?" I ask, waving the folded paper. The flag of information that could colonize River Bronswell's career and bleed it dry. Don't get me wrong, I could gorge food coma–inducing amounts of schadenfreude at the sight of River's demise. And after the Nexus Radio Lounge incident, I did. But this sounds next-level insidious.

She responds with a chuckle and a condescending sneer.

"Besides," I pause and toss the paper onto the counter. "I ain't down for going to jail."

"So you'll settle for letting him live in the cell block of your mind. Pathetic."

She hops off the barstool and prances toward me. My back slams into the fridge, and that better not be my bottle of vodka that toppled over. Her breath warms my cheek. A year and a half ago, I'd make a passive-aggressive comment about her lack of social distancing.

But not now.

Her breath smells oddly familiar. Watermelon and mint. It reminds me of Bobbi, and now I don't mind Lyla being all up in my space. She traces a finger along my temple and down the side of my face. Her nail is dagger-sharp. She could plunge it into my jugular at any moment and drink from the fountain of AC. I should be scared, but I'm obsessed with knowing how the hell she conducts her daily human tasks with nails like that. Putting clothes on, tying shoes, and personal hygiene. Her finger arrives at my chin. The sparkle in her eyes has me thinking she might slash my neck after all.

"AC, darling," she mutters into my ear. Her voice is both soothing and frightening. Her tongue slithers over her lower lip and she nibbles down. "This is the only way to set us both free."

"Us?"

I wiggle myself from between her and the fridge. Two feet away, next to my knife drawer, is the perfect place for self-defense purposes. Just in case. You should see her eyes. Laser focused, yet zombie-like. And this exchange has me wondering if her employers know a psycho has access to their company's data.

"I'm the biggest River Bronswell fan," she says indignantly.

"You made it clear that Bobbi weighs more, so technically, she—"

"Whatever," she interrupts. "You know what I mean."' I don't know what any of this means.

"You show up to my place, unannounced." I say, pacing around my apartment while she maintains eye contact without blinking. "And that..." I point to the piece of paper at the bar. "That seems wrong in so many ways, and how did you stumble across that information in the first place?"

Lyla crosses her arms and pouts. "Do I need to repeat myself, Mr. Cortes?" "A good IT gal always gets what she wants, *blah blah blah*."

I sit on my couch and bury my face in my hands.

"*Ewww*. Butt sweat," she says from behind. I should turn around and keep an eye on her. For safety's sake.

"My couch, my butt sweat. Deal with it," I mumble. "Besides, I'm dry now, if you must know."

Her hands land on my shoulders. She's obviously learned a thing or two from Bobbi. "Yeah, you're dry alright."

I stand up and face her. "Can't do this."

She hops the couch and plants herself in front of me. Two fists latch onto my shirt and tug me down so I'm on top of her. Her legs wrap around my torso, and this has escalated way too quickly.

"Can't do what?" she purrs. "This?"

Her lips part, and she plunges her tongue into my mouth. It swirls in and out. Wet, silky strokes paint my face. I taste the watermelon mint.

Bobbi's the bigger River fan, but Lyla's the better kisser. The scent of her shampoo shoots into my nose. Eucalyptus and cucumber, I think. She wrestles her way on top of me. Her hands clamp down on my wrists. She has made me an inmate in my own apartment, and at this moment, I don't mind.

Turning away from Lyla's mouth is harder than running with a hangover on the day after getting dumped by your girlfriend for a world-famous musician at a concert in front of the world. Her mouth smears against my cheek as I pull back.

"Can't do this, either," I say.

"Well," she says, dismounting me. "If you're gonna lead me on, then the least you can do is work with me."

I sit up and stare in the direction of the paper on the bar. My eyes narrow; they home in on Lyla. We stare at each other, then at the paper on the bar.

"No way in hell what's on that paper is true."

"Obsession can lead you to spaces you never knew possible," she replies.

Maybe she is the biggest River Bronswell fan.

Her gaze locks me in. I clutch a throw pillow and hold it to my chest. "Listen," she continues, running a pinky finger along her chin. "We can do this together, or I can go it alone, but this will be a lot easier if you just give in to your anger and help me out." I've already given in to my anger.

192

My version of giving in to anger generally involves pizza binges and spiking River's latte with a vomit-inducing elixir. "What do you expect me to do with this?"

"Read it."

I've already read it, and it sounds even more illegal than my previous stunt. I shake my head and hold my eyes closed, hoping that she'll change her mind and leave when I open them. I open my eyes, and she's still there.

"You expect me to slander him for what happened the other night?"

She mouths something I can't understand. A witch's curse, for all I know. She huffs and flails her arms in the air before smacking them down on her thighs. "He took your girlfriend, but your girlfriend took River from me."

"I didn't know he was yours in the first place."

She swings her legs onto my lap. Part of me hopes for another kiss, and part of me fears she'll strangle me with her legs. Like something out of a James Bond movie. A perfectly manicured toe circles my stomach and chest. "He'll never know it's me. It'll ruin him, but I can be there to pick up the pieces."

"Assuming you ever get near Bobbi and River again," I reply.

Her foot presses down on my chest. "Bobbi says you give the best foot rubs."

I press a fist to my mouth, a failed attempt to ignore her. She snakes her foot under my arms and presses a foot into the palm of my hand. I yank it away.

"Definitely can't do this."

"But you can stick your tongue in my mouth," she fires back. "Got it." She holds up three fingers, the "okay" sign.

"Actually, you shoved your tongue in my mouth," I reply. "Besides, how do I know you didn't make up what's on that sheet of paper you pulled out of your bra?"

The next ten minutes are a rehashing of a mandatory course on cybersecurity. The scams, the phishing, the ransomware. All it takes is patience, persistence, and the right target and hackers can get anything they want, whenever they want, and from whoever they want.

"River's mom never knew what hit her," says Lyla.

"So you installed ransomware in her laptop. River's family paid up, and you still kept their files?" I turn to the paper again. Then back to Lyla. "All because you're his biggest fan, and he's the love of your life. That's believable."

"Yes on all accounts," she says.

I take her foot and guide her leg down off my chest. I stand up and grab another pillow, squeezing it like I wish I could have squeezed River's head at the concert. Hard, but not fatally hard. "And when do you suppose is the right time for me to read about this $150 million COVID-19 settlement with employees of his record label?"

"Sooner rather than later."

The night of the concert plays back in my head. River taking shots with me and Bobbi. Bobbi undressing River with her eyes. River returning the favor. River inviting Bobbi on stage. River dedicating that stupid song to Bobbi. River kissing Bobbi and Bobbi returning the favor. River and Bobbi making a fool out of me in front of thousands. Hundreds of thousands more on the internet.

Tears of anger and embarrassment pour out of my sockets. Seeing River hunched over gave me something I never thought possible: a desire for rage and to see him suffer more. The only thing my mouth can utter is the one thing Lyla wants me to utter. "Okay, I'm in."

CHAPTER 29

Weeks have passed since Bobbi left me, but it seems like an eternity. Her obsession with River should have been a red flag flapping in my face, telling me to abandon ship. My obsession with getting back at River has made me forget that I ever enjoyed dating her.

I stroll into Cade's office, trying to keep the schadenfreude to a minimum. "Any word from River's people?" I ask, even though I have no shits to give. "He was in pretty bad shape."

Cade spins his chair around and smacks his feet to the floor. "Skip says he'll recover. Probably spoiled coffee creamer." They have no idea. Cade leans forward, elbows on his desk. He folds his hands in a managerial way. The way a human resources manager would tell someone to pack their crap in a box and wait for security to escort them out of the building. He sighs. "This is your friend talking, not your supervisor."

He taps the tips of his fingers on each other, then lays his chin on the palm of a hand. "I just don't understand how you can be so angry at River but feel nothing of the sort for Bobbi." He'll never understand me. Nobody will.

He stands and walks behind me. Now it's a preshow interrogation. Answer his questions or face the consequences. The fluorescent lights are the lone spotlights, the ones you see in those old detective movies. Cade grabs the chair next to me and spins it around, just like one of those tough-guy detectives with the cheap department store suits that are two sizes too big and held up by suspenders that don't match. But instead of a cigar, Cade's vaping.

I'm being interrogated by my friend who smells like cotton candy, deejay fog, and a stripper with daddy issues.

He asks if I've talked to her since the incident, if we've traded texts or Facebook messages. He asks if she's called the request line. He wants to know what I'd tell her if she calls.

No.

No.

I unfriended her.

Not that I know of, but nobody bothers to call the request line anymore.

To screw off.

Cade's grin suggests he approves of my sentiments and that he shares them with me. "Turns out, you may have a chance to tell her in person," he says.

"Huh?"

"Tomorrow's a big day," he says, blowing vape smoke into the air.

"You're gonna give up vaping, and the building will no longer smell like a strip club?"

"You'll be announcing the next Nexus Flyaway," he replies.

"And?"

"You'll be escorting a listener to the Global Music Awards, where they'll interview River Bronswell on Radio Row."

Before I can object, he says, "Because you're the nationally syndicated personality on staff and there will be fans from your other affiliate stations in attendance."

I fail to understand why the station would put me and River in yet another volatile situation. But I approve of their folly.

His interrogation continues. "You're an entertainer, and this is entertaining. It's a real-life soap opera."

"But this is my life we're talking about. And in case you forgot, we're friends and you're supposed to have my back."

Cade strolls back to the chair behind his computer. "We are friends, but I'm also your program director." Then he goes on a diatribe about how important it is to leave ourselves out in the open for our listeners. How this is what separates Nexus Radio from the pretenders. How his hands are tied because it's a directive from corporate. He's nonstop with his propaganda.

"Think about how this will motivate and inspire our listeners to demand more," he says. "How you'll be an example."

"Of how to keep getting shit on. Beautiful," I say.

"Of how you're a fighter," he says. His eyes beam with excitement. "You'll win hearts and minds. Think of all the listeners who heard the harrowing tale of AC getting ditched for River Bronswell.

"Think about how, rather than choose sides, they hear you be the bigger man, as you have been through this entire ordeal. Think about all those people listening that will have breakup envy. The ones thinking about how lucky you, River, and Bobbi are. So lucky that you can be in the same room together, conversing with one another without anyone having to call the cops."

"Yeah, so lucky."

"You don't realize it now," he says. "But you will."

"I won't."

Cade blathers about this interview at the Global Music Awards. How it's going to drive listenership through the roof. And how it's going to be the best thing to happen to Nexus Radio since the day I met Bobbi.

"Really?"

"Yes," he replies.

But then it hits me. I have an in. And now it's time for me to cash another check my rage-addicted ass has already written.

CHAPTER 30

In radio, the media platform that haters say is dying, one thing can drive ratings through the roof. Anything having to do with River Bronswell. It should not surprise anyone that in a day and age where people buy packages of fast-food condiments on eBay or pieces of fruit duct taped to a wall for $120,000, fans of River would pay any price for anything having to do with him.

Nexus Radio once gave away a coffee cup used by River before his first stadium performance, authenticated by a picture of Biggs and Sasha posing with him and the cup. Shortly after, Biggs hocked a giant loogie and spit in it. Sasha made sure to get a pic for Nexus Radio's private files. *Shhh…*don't tell anyone.

As I gather notes about the trip, I think about the listener who messaged my show last year, thanking the station for the tickets to the River concert. She had just moved into an apartment after getting kicked out of her parents' house for dropping out of school to start a clothing line. Three days after she moved in, still unpacked, the apartment complex caught fire, and she narrowly escaped. She lost everything, including her cat and her sewing machines. But this one experience provided a glimmer of something she had lost forever—hope. Hope that good things can happen to good people after bad things happen to them. For a moment, her story gives me hope. But she probably hopes River will propose to Bobbi and invite me to the wedding. And then I think about the Nexus Lounge and how that's just an appetizer of misery for Mr. Bronswell.

With headphones and a stack of papers wrapped around a bottle of water in hand, I head down the halls of Nexus Studio. I walk past plaque after plaque, gold record after gold record, and platinum record after platinum record. Accolades commemorating the likes of Dua Lipa, Jason Derulo, and Usher. Signed jeans worn by Mariah Carey. A signed bra for breast cancer awareness month that never got authenticated because the artist refused to have her picture taken while signing it. An autographed Union Jack flag signed by Sting. This hallway should serve as a constant reminder that even on my worst day, I am lucky. That I'm not stuck in some mundane desk job, doomed to eight hours in a cube farm baking under fluorescent lights, surrounded by fake plants and faker colleagues. But it doesn't.

I set my headphones down on the cold marble countertop next to the phones. They're still lit up from Biggs and Sasha's announcement that I have about the biggest Nexus Flyaway in history. They name-dropped the world's biggest artist. They teased that one lucky listener will get to interview him. They predict a 100 percent chance of drama when all is said and done.

Nexus pushed out tune-in notifications to listen for my announcement, which included River's blurred-out face with a caption at the bottom. The average Nexus listener wouldn't be able to decipher who the blurred face belongs to. But the average River fan could. Someone on our digital team accidentally—or accidentally on purpose—forgot to blur out the tattoo on River's left wrist, the Japanese word for live, 暮らす, and it caused an avalanche of messages. It flooded our email system, crashed the Nexus website, and jammed our request lines. Hundreds of tweets, Facebook comments, and Instagram posts inundated our social platforms every hour.

We got offers from listeners willing to sell their kidneys. Listeners threatening to cut off their baby sister's hair and perform black magic. And listeners willing to swim through hot liquid magma. Their empty promises amuse us, even though they swear by their allegiance.

I unwrap my printouts from around my water bottle. The condensation makes the bottom paper stick. I place the partially soggy sheets on the stand in front of me, clipping them with a tiny black clip. I untangle my headphones and turn to the counter on the screen. Sixty seconds to break. Sixty seconds until I announce the trip of a lifetime.

The headphone cord continues to challenge my patience. I feed the adapter through each curl, as if I'm a hairstylist working a barrette through a model's perm.

Thirty seconds.

The halls of Nexus Radio are better than any rock 'n' roll museum, with oversized statues of movie characters.

The River Bronswell cutout stares at me from the corner. His smug grin. The one that pesters me with petulance. The grin that I'd love to slap into next century. The cutout that I'd love to drive a pair of scissors through but don't because it belongs to Sasha. He torments me, but he'll get his.

Twenty seconds.

The cord unravels. I wrap my headphones around my ears. I clear my throat. I pound the mic button on. My finger glides the volume up.

The Nexus Radio halls are so much cooler than any rock 'n' roll museum because without these halls and this moment and this trip, I wouldn't have the opportunity to see River again and make him pay for what he did to me in front of his fans and the world—and on behalf of anyone who's experienced anything like what I've experienced.

This will make the Nexus Lounge debacle look like a cakewalk, and the @muzikstan21 look like amateur hour.

CHAPTER 32

"Think about that one time you heard me or some other Nexus Radio deejay interview an artist, and you thought you could ask better questions."

I pause for a split second to give a snarky look into my smartphone camera recording video of the announcement for social media. "Now is your chance to ask away because you'll be my VIP guest sidekick at the Global Music Awards in Hollywood. And as my sidekick, you'll interview the one and only River Bronswell. All you have to do is listen to win a framed and autographed River poster and the trip of a lifetime." I glance at the counter on the monitor. Another flawlessly timed break. I push the button to start the next song. "And speaking of the world's biggest star, here's River with 'Go Get Yours'...which you will when you win at four o'clock today!"

———————

I answer the request lines.

"I'm calling about the River trip," says a voice from line one.

"When are you giving away the Nexus trip? I missed the details," pleads a voice from line seven.

"I heard you all have a trip to see my future ex," declares a voice from line four.

"River is my life. I must have that trip," shouts a voice from line nine.

Coming up at five 'til four.

Three fifty-five.

In about fifty-one minutes.

Keep listening.

Joy radiates from the phone lines. "I've seen River fifteen times in the past four years," says a proud voice from line three.

"I'd leave my boyfriend for River so he can ditch your ex-girlfriend," says a voice on line eight.

"I'll trade you my three-year-old brother for that trip," says line five.

"I would set my house on fire if I knew you'd give me that trip," says line two.

"I would cyberstalk everyone who ever harassed you on Twitter if you give me that trip," says another voice on line seven.

The phones are too much to handle, and I don't bother with the text screen and social media.

"Fifteen times? Cool."

"Don't leave your boyfriend yet."

"I'm sure your parents approve."

"Put the matches away."

"Hmmm...definitely rooting for you."

Cade tells me not to run any of the calls on the air. Something about inciting violence.

"Can't say he doesn't deserve it," I say with a grin. He definitely does.

"Yes, he stole your girlfriend, but get a grip, dude."

"What should I grip?" I huff.

"I can't have you encouraging this kind of behavior," says Cade.

"Okay, maybe the arson call crossed a line," I say. But I don't mean it.

Cade rolls up the chair next to the phone lines. "So did the one about cyberstalking."

"But it was hilarious."

Cade tisks, then rolls his eyes. "So hilarious."

"Sometimes I think you lost your sense of humor when you got the program director job," I say.

"Sometimes I think you're asking for management to have me fire one of my closest friends."

I pick up my headphones to prepare for my next break. I slide them over my head, covering only one ear. We stare each other down. He huffs and walks to the door, grabs the handle and says, "Don't do anything stupid."

"Don't do anything stupid" is Cade speak for "I won't be listening because I'll be in a meeting, so have at it but don't lose the license."

Challenge accepted. The hardest part is deciding which listener from this cornucopia of callers I should run first.

Contest time has arrived. Who will join me when I reveal to the world River's transgressions? Will they turn on him and join the internet mob of maniacs who will surely shame him into the forgotten land of has-beens? Or will they turn on me?

I adjust the mic to my mouth and pound the mic button on. "It's AC on Nexus Radio and the time is now for you to text 'River' to 11-11-11...if you do and you're the 111th person in, you'll win a trip to the Global Music Awards as my guest, where you'll interview the one and only River Bronswell!"

Lyla's information marinates in the back of my mind as I refresh the text screen. Ten seconds after my solicit, we arrive at the 111th text. The number looks familiar, but all the numbers look the same when dozens of them are on the screen at the same time.

I pick up the phone and call. It rings once, and the voice on the other line sounds familiar. "Hello?!?" the voice yelps. She breathes hard into the phone. Like someone who hasn't exercised in two years and just climbed a flight of stairs.

"This is AC from Nexus Radi—"

She squeals. The frequency of her voice tickles my eardrums. It might be blood. I should sue. "Tell me I won," she screams over and over.

"You won!" I reply. And I can't wait to shatter River's world in front of her. It'll be like the first time I took my parents to see their favorite band, Maroon 5. Glorious.

The voice on the other end of the phone, between heavy breaths and shouting, babbles about the chance to finally meet her man. As her voice calms to a conversational tone, it sounds more familiar with every word she speaks.

"I can't help but wonder," I say. "What's the first question you'll ask River when you meet him at the Global Music Awards?"

"How long were you sick after the Nexus Lounge incident?"

A woman after my heart. "Too soon," I reply but don't mean it. And I hope he spent the entire night bowed before the porcelain god, chomping down pills of Pepto. "Pick another question."

"I'd be a fool to not ask why he did what he did with Bobbi on the night of the concert," she replies. And the rasp of the listener's voice haunts me.

"Some things are better left unasked," I retort. And now she has me fired up and wanting to forget Lyla's plan and treat River to another Ipecac latte. "Hey, all this excitement, and I never even asked your name."

The voice on the other end of the phone giggles. "Oh, AC."

"Your name is O-A-C?" I ask.

"This is Lyla."

No way it's *the* Lyla.

"Hello?" she rasps.

"*Sooooooo...*" I pause. "Lyla, you working today?"

"Of course, but a good IT girl always gets what she wants," she says. "So I convinced my boss to let me take a long break just so I could try and win. And it worked!"

"Well congratulations," I say, and how in the world did she, of all people, end up being the one to win this? "Hold on for a moment and I'll take your information off the air."

"Thank you, AC and THANK YOU, NEXUS RADIO!"

The universe has a strange way of arranging itself.

CHAPTER 33

Flying in an airplane for the first time since before the pandemic reminds me how much I hate airplanes. But five hours in a cylindrical can of farticles and body odor next to a screaming toddler is a small price to pay to see River's demise. My phone beeps as I worm through LAX. I stop. I fish it out of my back pocket. Lyla. *Hi Aubrey, I see you. Meet me at Starby's? Coffee on me!*

I look up. She does see me. About twenty yards ahead, she waves me down as she stands in front of a register at Starbucks. Her blue hair matches that of the barista behind the register and complements the purple hair of the barista calling out names from behind the espresso machine. "Order for Larry," she barks with a voice deeper than mine.

The circle motion Lyla makes with her hands gets bigger and bigger with every step I take. "C'mon, Aubrey," she commands. "The line's not getting any shorter, and we're not getting any younger." C'mon Aubrey? She patronizes me the way a mom summons her school-aged son to hurry up because momma just wants to get home and binge watch *General Hospital* while gorging down a bag of Cheetos.

I get to the counter and her perfume hits me in the face as she comes in for a hug. She wears the same perfume as Bobbi, and now I know she's messing with me. "So, what'll you have, Mr. Cortes? I already ordered."

"I'll have what she's having, thank you," I reply.

We shuffle ourselves to the side of the store. Her River Bronswell suitcase bumps into my leg. "A picture of River Bronswell on a suitcase, holding a suitcase with a picture of River Bronswell on a suitcase in one hand—"

"And a mug with a picture of me in the other, yes," interrupts Lyla, smiling down at her luggage. Her eyes seem glazed over.

"That's...interesting."

"Took my friend about a month to finish it," she quips.

The barista calls out from behind the counter. "River Bronswell's favorite Starbucks customers!"

I lower my head. And this must be what it felt like when Daniel LaRusso's mother's car broke down in *Karate Kid*. We gather our drinks and luggage and scurry to the next to nearest table. "What are the odds, Lyla?'"

She peers into my eyes and lifts her chin. Her smile is a thin line that shows no teeth. "Odds?" She lifts her drink to her mouth.

"Yes," I reply. "The odds that the person who gave me this—" I pause and pull the pink piece of paper from my shirt pocket and slap it on the table. "Seems unlikely that the only person besides River and his people that know about this would be the one who'd win a contest where she can meet him." Lyla's eyes shift down toward the table. I swipe the paper and shove it back into my shirt pocket.

"A good IT girl always gets what she wants," she purrs. And she raises her eyebrows as if what she wants is me and not the chance to meet River. Her tongue slithers across her lower lip.

"What does that mean?

"Everything," growls Lyla. She sips her latte. Swirling it in little circles, she takes a huge gulp and leans toward me. Her low-cut blouse droops onto the table. Her beaded necklace knocks gently on the tabletop. She huddles herself closer, squeezing her arms inward to create cleavage I refuse to look at. "Don't you wanna know how good I am?"

I refuse eye contact and home in on the huge digital banner to my left. A Global Music Awards ad with blinking Hollywood-style letters and a shadowed pic of River Bronswell's profile, singing into a mic amid a sea of hands. I can't escape him. But soon, he won't escape me. "Okay, Lyla, enlighten me," I say. "How good are you?"

She puckers her lips and rears herself back, crossing her arms. And she lets me have it. She says a good IT girl knows how to hack into anything she wants. But will only use her knowledge for good. Not bad. That she could easily hack into bank accounts, credit card accounts. Scamming old people into co-signing on auto loans is for amateurs. And people with no purpose. But she has a purpose, and she sounds crazier than me when I hatched my Ipicac plan. Her purpose is River. And convincing him that she's the one he belongs with. Not Bobbi.

Lyla giggles. "Don't just look at me like that. Say something."

"It's just," I struggle to find the words. "How..."

"Easily," she says.

Lyla tells me she's friends with a guy who works at the company that runs our phone system. Everybody knows somebody, she says.

I slink down in my chair and pull my cap down.

Hacking a radio station's phone system is easier than a dimpled dame onstage at a River Bronswell show, she says.

I sigh.

"Too soon," she says. "Sorry."

Lyla pops the lid off her cup and digs a cube of ice out with her straw. Between crunches, she says, "So I made myself the winner."

"You can't just rig a contest," I say, feeling used. Snookered. I wanna call Cade, but that would make matters worse. He'd accuse me of conspiring with her. Of doing anything I can to get out of interviewing River. Of trying to get out of doing my job.

"Quit acting like a saint, Mr. Ipecac."

A hot heat rushes from my head and down my body. Coffee shoots up my throat. For a split second, I consider letting it shoot all over Lyla because maybe that'd scare her off, and I don't have to listen to her anymore. But I swallow hard, forcing it back down. My mouth hangs open, but words fail to come out.

"How do I know?" she asks. But her grin tells me she knows. "Because a good IT girl knows how to get what she wants."

My eyelids twitch. My hands throb. I look down and see them clinched into fists, red with rage.

"Oh, calm down, Aubrey.'"

"AC."

"Whatever," she says. She lays a hand on one of mine. I pull both of them back and shove them into the pocket of my hoodie.

"Did you hack my phone?"

"*Hack* sounds like such a pejorative when you say it, Aubrey," she replies, tapping a finger on the table. "Let's just say..." she slants her head and stares upward for a moment. "Let's just say I snuck into your phone to see if I could trust you."

"*Trust* seems like a strange word to use right now," I mumble. And she flashes me a stare that looks like she's ready to call the authorities. "Okay, so we both know something about each other," I continue. "But I meant it when I said I was all in on this."

"Oh, I know."

I huff. "Good."

"So, anything I need to know before the interview?" she asks.

"Security's tight. So travel lightly. No oversized bags, etcetera, etcetera."

She nods. "I'll bring nothing more than a River Bronswell pen and a notepad."

CHAPTER 34

If you ever go viral for singing an auto-tuned cover of a River
Bronswell song and substitute the ukulele with a xylophone, get a
manager. If you ever go viral for changing up rap lyrics so they're
preschool friendly? Get an agent. Because if you're lucky—like, hit the
lotto and end up on *The Today Show* and *The Wendy Williams Show* lucky
—then you can extend your fifteen minutes of fame to fifteen and a half
minutes. And if you're really lucky, then guest-starved producers at the
Global Music Awards will beg you to grace the dingy red carpet and to
chat with personalities on Radio Row. This is my office. My temporary
studio. A convention chock full of viral internet stars, d-listers, "that one
guy from that one show that aired for one season in the nineties," "that
one host from that one game show that ran in 2008," and an occasional
artist that people actually recognize without being prefaced with the
phrase "that one guy." Producers blanket the area with them, which
makes planning a show hard, especially when you've been selling the
sizzle of talking to the world's biggest stars.

Lyla and I navigate the blob of media personalities to get to our
booth. The fluorescent lighting provides an unwelcome reality check for

the ones who epitomize the term "face for radio." Especially me. An abyss of frosty tips, overpriced ripped jeans, fake eyelash extensions, hair extensions, and two-sizes-too-small shirts hinders my view of where we need to go. The sea of media personalities parts with just enough time for me to catch our logo on a table. "There," I tell Lyla, waving a finger in the direction of the table. "That's our table over there."

"I've never seen anything like this," she replies. "I knew River's demise would be special." She holds a hand to her heart. Shifting her head from side to side to check for eavesdroppers, she lowers her gaze and continues, leaning in toward me. "But I had no idea it would be this special."

"Well, let's hope he even shows up."

Our position in the room commands the most space, but it's also in the back. So by the time anyone—especially actual musicians relevant to Nexus Radio—gets to us, they are exhausted and bored.

"This'll have to do, but they've got to stop putting us in the back," I say, setting my duffle bag down on the floor next to the table. "They do this every year—and every year, we get shorted at least four interviews."

I turn to Lyla, who's wide-eyed and fascinated by the hustle and bustle of the area, and I say, "So this is how it'll work. River will arrive at around 3:30. Which, in River time, is 4:30. Which is about an hour from the start of red-carpet coverage. Which will not give us much time with him." Lyla nods. Then we go over the list of the Global Music Awards list of do's and dont's for the media junket.

Do not flirt with the artists, a tall order for Lyla.

Do not argue with or provoke the artists, an order that I can't wait for Lyla and me to violate.

Do not touch the artists. Lyla rears her head back and mumbles, "But I wanna give him a hug. He's always so touchy-feely whenever he's with his fans—"

"DO NOT TOUCH THE ARTISTS."

Do not ask talent to pose with anything containing a logo. "Sounds like we're not allowed to do anything," says Lyla.

"We can kiss their asses," I reply. "And tell them how lost the world would be without their art."

Lyla grumbles. She sets her purse down on the table. It's another hand-crafted River Bronswell purse with his likeness depicted in the style of Andy Warhol. She grabs her smartphone and lifts it up for a selfie. "Well, I still think this will be fun," she says with a diabolical grin as her eyes sink back into her head. "Especially the part where we ask him about the party."

"Yeah," I reply. I pull up a chair and offer it to her. She accepts. I sit next to her. "About that."

Lyla rests her arms on her legs and forms a steeple with her hands. Her eyebrows curl toward each other. One of them rises, encouraging me to continue.

"Let's start off with a few easy questions first," I reply. "Then, once we establish a rapport and he realizes—" I pause and make air finger quotes. "Realizes that he's in friendly territory and I won't badger him about what happened the night of the concert or whether or not he banged my ex before the interview," I continue. "That's when we hit 'em with the goods."

Lyla replies with a series of nods. Short ones, then a couple of long, deep nods, a green light to continue.

"But I have to know, Lyla," I continue. I scan the area to ensure nobody overhears. "Are you sure you wanna go through with this?"

She inhales a long breath and slides back in her chair. "This," she answers as she extends her hands in the air and wiggles her fingers. "This, as in ruin his night, maybe his year, and if the stars align in our favor, his career? Yes."

"That's nice, but—" I say, pausing and extending my neck over the crowd to see if anyone I know, namely Cade, is approaching the table. It'd be a shame if he snuck up on us, overheard our plan for River, and toe-tagged it before we ever got started. I let out a long breath. "But aren't you at least a little worried about your friendship with Bobbi?"

Lyla tells me not to care about her friendship with Bobbi. To worry about my job dismantling River's career. To supplant a deadly virus in his life that will colonize his head and live there rent-free forever. Somehow, this sounds worse than putting Ipecac in his coffee. And somehow, I like it.

My phone buzzes. It's Cade.

What I hear Cade telling me on the phone is what I hear River's fans telling me in unison: "Don't do anything stupid."

The stopper of stupidity reminds me of the one time and last time he had ever done anything stupid with an artist. Something about getting busted by the cops for buying weed for an unnamed rapper. They said they'd let him off the hook if he brought them backstage to the Christmas show where he was to bring the devil's lettuce. The five-0 fanboys went in, ready for selfies but in uniform. The rapper got paranoid because he had a coffee table covered in ganga. He pulled a gun in self-defense and the cops pulled theirs, too, but Cade managed to deescalate the situation with his gift of gab. But not before the rapper and his entourage ditched out before performing, which caused a riot at Lecnac Grove Arena, a few dozen arrests, and some unsavory publicity on the local news.

"You've been through a lot, and I'm starting to worry that maybe you and your ex's best friend interviewing the guy who stole her from you might be the thing to set you over the edge," he says.

Oh, so now he's worried. Took him long enough. But that's okay because my being okay will be the last thing he'll be thinking about once Lyla and I finish with River.

As I sit in an overpriced café down the hall from Radio Row, I listen to him lecture me, coach me, baby me, and threaten me. My superpower is tuning out my boss, even though he's one of my best friends.

"Lilian's up my ass, and I thought for sure I'd be able to get away without going to that godforsaken town," he says.

I take a sip of my latte, scoping out the collection of Roman emperors hanging on the wall across from me. "This is amazing," I say, smacking my lips. "This is the best latte I've ever had. You'll love it. Nutty and strong, but not too—"

"Did you hear anything I just said?" he asks, annoyed.

"Something about our boss up your ass."

"I'll be there soon to make sure you don't do anything—"

"Stupid, I know," I interrupt.

He squawks something unintelligible and clears his throat. He slams his phone, freeing me of his castigation.

I gaze around the café. Plumes of smoke dance into the air from the coffee machines. The constant whirl of voices. The banging of plates and mugs from the back. The bright green statue of some Caesar-looking dude stares at me. Even the statue of a Roman emperor at the café judges me. If looks could speak, it would say, "Listen to your boss and don't do anything stupid." The tightly clenched lips on his face give off an air of disdain. His slightly raised head looks down on me. In his day, he'd likely have me killed. Thrown into a colosseum with a gladiator—or worse. Maybe a gladiator and a couple of caged lions. With no weapons, other than my scrawny arms.

Don't do anything stupid.

That's what Cade, River's fans, and the judgy emperor are telling me.

What started as a plot against River because of Bobbi has morphed into a twisted obsession with teaching River a lesson in front of the world that adores him.

I circle my spoon inside my overpriced bowl of fruit parfait. I lift the spoonful of yogurt and fruit. My teeth clench. Blueberry juice squirts into the back of my throat. Only revenge will taste sweeter. River's wretched fandom has me relying on the morphine of their madness. What Lyla and I have planned will shatter their precious image of him. They'll turn on

Lyla and me, no doubt. I'll get canceled by the fandom, the culture, and our listeners. And I'll likely get fired.

I take another sip of my latte.

But I'd rather get fired than let rage live in my head because I need the closure.

CHAPTER 35

As I check the mic levels and battery power on my mic and fumble around with the stack of notes for the interview, the one that will banish River Bronswell into a black hole of irrelevance, he appears. His walk makes me want to stomp my foot on his newspaper-boy hat, then remove it from his head and stuff it down his throat. But two bodyguards stand on each side of him, and there goes my chance. Oh well. Wait a second...

Where's Bobbi? What is she doing? Was she so peeved that he's wearing a faded Nirvana concert T-shirt—he was only two-years old at the height of their success—that this level of shallowness was too much to handle?

Or maybe she's up in his hotel room, probably recovering from an all-nighter. The greatest sex imaginable.

Ewwww—stop.

We lock eyes, and he turns away because that's what scumbags do. They avoid eye contact.

I turn to Lyla—her face is buried in her phone. She squeals and squeaks like a dog toy. Her eyes bounce up from her camera and down at the screen of her smartphone, trying to balance the vision of St. Bronswell in real life and the perfect angle.

"Remember, five minutes. At four and a half, his manager will wave a finger in the air. That means we need to wrap up," I say.

"And remember the rules," she replies with a tinge of sarcasm. She makes air quotes with a free hand and whispers, "the rules we're about to break."

"I like you," I reply, admiring the way she puffs her lips as she investigates her lipstick in the reflection of her River-themed compact. And aside from her obvious obsession, I do like her. Maybe after this, we can go on and create our own little spin-off love story, rooted in retribution. Sasha's right. I do get attached quickly.

"Oh, AC," she scoffs. "That's adorable." The tone in her voice dismisses me the way a grade-school teacher dismisses a boy who gives her his mom's half-empty bottle of perfume for Christmas. As if she never plunged her tongue into my mouth and straddled me like a prize-winning stallion back at my place. Whatever.

River, flanked by Skip, and a couple of menacingly large bodyguards, continues to traverse Radio Row. I crane my neck, searching for any sign of Bobbi. Nothing. Only fellow DJs, their producers, and an occasional listener tag-along like Lyla. The pathway between booths is a human web of limbs. They peel off with each step he takes. Then more latch on.

"I'll handle the introduction and the first three questions, then you're in charge for a couple of minutes," I tell Lyla. "This gives us about four minutes."

She lifts her head and lowers her eyelids. "And what happens at the four-minute mark?"

I scour the crowd for signs of River—and Bobbi. He's about ten yards away. Still no signs of Bobbi. She's probably writing a fanfic about their amazing romp in the sheets last night, and now I can't wait to spend an entire paycheck on a stack of books and toss them in a Bobbi Falstaff bonfire. I hold up a forefinger. "This is the sign for one minute left." I circle my fingers around each other like a bingo cage. "And this means we need to wrap it up."

"He's done tons of interviews, so he knows the cue. Once he stops, I'll jump in with the slam dunk," I explain. I knock on the table and give her a thumbs up. "And don't be nervous—he's a human just like us." A flaming dumpster fire of a human who's about to get what he deserves.

I flick the switch on the processors and radio in to our producers back at the station. Covering the mics with my hands, I whisper, "The mics are hot. Which means they're on, so anything from this point on is subject to getting put on the air and online."

River, Skip, and his crew approach the table. Still no sign of Bobbi, and now I'm certain she's huddled in the corner of that overpriced café with a bedazzled River Bronswell notebook, writing about last night's tryst. I hope the fangirls on WattPad trash it and cancel it.

You could drive a truck through Lyla's smile, and I'd like to drive a truck through River. That'd make me smile. "This is amazing," she says.

"AC," says Skip firmly, extending a hand. I accept. Our grip tightens for a second. We hold a steady eye, and it reminds me of the time Stone Cold Steve Austin and Shane-O-Mac shook hands. How I'd love to pull him in and finish him off with a Stone Cold Stunner.

"Skip," I say. I turn to the pop music messiah-about-to-turn-pariah. "River, nice to see you again."

I once learned how facial muscles indicate a fake smile. The risorius ones pull the sides down, so says my dad. River hasn't unlearned his unfortunate trait. He extends a hand. I refuse and use my head to show him his seat.

"Thanks," he says.

"And this is Lyla, our Nexus Flyaway winner, and she'll conduct most of the inter—"

Lyla plows through me with the force of a professional linebacker pursuing a loose football, River being said football. I catch an elbow to the ribcage and am sure something cracked. Maybe the cracked rib will poke an internal organ, cause me to hemorrhage, and then some EMTs can wheel me the hell out of here because loose-cannon Lyla's behavior is giving me doubts.

"OH MY GOD, MAY I GIVE YOU A HUG?" she exclaims with the happiness of a snot-nosed six-year-old meeting a fake-bearded mall Santa. Before he could give Lyla an answer, the two are cheek-to-cheek. His lips are squeezed and puckered like fish lips.

Skip flashes a grin, patting Lyla on the back and guiding her back to her seat. And we start. "All access to the Global Music Awards continues with me, AC, and our Nexus Flyway Winner. Her name is Lyla. Lyla, how are you feeling?"

Lyla gathers enough composure to sob-shout a couple of words. "I'm so—"

But she's breathing so hard, a sea-green slimeball plays whack-a-mole in her nose, so she stops before she can say anything else. I hand her a tissue, she blows her nose, and continues, "I'm so excited!"

"If you're on our Instagram feed, you'll see that Lyla's speechless and crying happy tears because she's about to interview our next guest, River Bronswell."

Lyla wipes her eye, smearing pink and gray from her eye makeup down her face, turning her into a creepy, sad clown face meme.

"I'll be fine," she says.

"Thanks for inviting me back to the Nexus airwaves," says River. "This appearance will go far better than the previous one, if you know what I mean."

I know exactly what he means. And it will go better, but not for him.

"We share a storied past. It's the least we can do for one of music's most treasured artists," I reply.

River homes in on Lyla's bag. His eyes widen. "This is...interesting," he quips, stroking his chin.

The two exchange words about her handmade purse. Three hours to find the right image on Google. About six hours to hand draw the design. And a little more than five thousand beads.

"So as you can tell, Lyla has a slight obsession," I say. Not "leave your-boyfriend for River Bronswell on stage" obsessed. But obsessed.

Lyla and River chuckle. "But don't worry, she's not 'carve your face off and wear it as a mask' obsessed." Just "ruin your career" obsessed. That's all.

Lyla shoves an elbow into my arm.

"What?" I reply, clutching my fragile, almost nonexistent muscle. River's blank stare indicates he's not into my jokes.

"Enough of the pleasantries, Lyla, whatcha got for River?" She unfolds a pink sheet of paper and clears her throat. But my attention focuses elsewhere. On the final question. I imagine his pathetic little pouty face. And Skip and his two rent-a-cops escorting his miserable carcass back to his hotel room, where he'll drown in a River of his own tears, rendering him useless to perform before a national audience. And when fans ask what happened, the truth will set us free and send him into pop-music purgatory.

"Would you rather perform for Bach or Beethoven?"

Who are those guys?

"Which dead president would you like to perform for?"

JFK. The womanizingest womanizer to ever live in the White House. Obvious pick.

"If you could smash your ukulele over anyone's head, who would it be?

Finally, a good one. I love that Skip didn't bother to screen our questions before the interview.

Word vomit, incoming. "Can he pick himself?" I ask.

River's mouth drops open, and my fist would look great in it. Taylor Swift's "I Can't Believe I Won" face is more believably shocked. He acts as though the Lecnac Arena concert never happened.

I look past him, ignoring his answer. Time is my focus.

"Tell me about the night you met Bobbi," says Lyla.

The pungent, vinegar-like flavor of bile shoots up and into my mouth. I power it back down, coughing and clearing my throat to make the burn go away. My head goes light for a split second, and I shake it off. Looking at the counter, I regain my composure. Her time has expired. And after this next question, so will River's.

CHAPTER 36

Lyla and I trade glances. Then she and River trade glances. Then River and I trade glances. A lump in my throat forces an awkward silence. More awkward than Biggs reading Bobbi's fanfic to Sasha during a staff meeting. Lyla cracks her knuckles. Her eyes bulge, growing to half the size of her face. She huffs. Why does it look as though she wants to stab me with her pen?

I shuffle my notes. They click on the table top as River's eyes shift from me to Lyla. Then to my notes. "So, Mr. Bronswell," I raise my chin and narrow my eyes.

"Mr. Cortes," he replies, tugging at the sleeve of his Nirvana concert T-shirt and I bet he can't even name a song other than "Smells Like Teen Spirit" or "All Apologies." He pisses on Kurt Cobain's legacy by wearing it.

"A reliable source informed me," I pause and raise my eyebrows at Lyla. Her face is bright pink. A vein snakes up to the surface of her forehead. It distracts me so much, this little snake pulsating next to her penciled-in eyebrow. Lyla grabs my hand and stabs it with her pen.

"Nobody informed you of anything!" she shouts. She stands above me and yanks the pen out of my hand. The pain is worse than anything I've ever experienced, except for having to watch *General Hospital* with my mom as a kid.

"What the—" River shoots out of his chair and takes a few steps back, falling down the stairs leading up to our table. He squirms about the floor, crawling away from the area. Wriggling about like a teenager fleeing a killer in a horror movie, he grabs hold of one of his bodyguards' pant legs.

One and a half gallons of blood flow through the average human. And it looks as though three and a half gallons are shooting out of my hand.

"What are you doing?" I shout, grasping my bleeding hand, blood trickling through my fingers and down my arms.

"This is for my brother!" she shouts.

I'm too busy trying to not freak out at the sight of my blood to notice Lyla ramming a pen into my neck.

My body collapses to the ground, but not before my head slams on the corner of the broadcast table. "What do you—" I moan, grabbing my neck. It burns with pain. "What do you mean, your brother?" I ask.

She hovers over me. Arms crossed, she growls, "My brother Stan Stansfield. You might recognize him as @muzikstan21 on Twitter."

My eyes flutter. Two Lylas appear before me. Two too many. And now I need one of River's hired goons to remove her. And a medical professional to remove this pen from my neck.

Lyla's voice is muffled and slow. Like we're in a tunnel. A tunnel of terror as she slams a foot down on my chest. She laughs. "My brother lost his job because of you and the deep fakes you mailed to his boss, you son of a bitch."

"I—"

She hoists her foot in the air and slams it into my chest again. And it sucks that River's rent-a-cops haven't done shit yet. "You have nothing of value to add to this conversation," she says. "Everything you touch turns to shit. You shit stain. My brother was a decent person. He got fired from the job he loved and nearly killed himself after your stunt."

"But...how—"

I stop as I brace myself for another stamp on the chest.

Lyla holds her foot up. Then stamps it down on the ground. She straddles me. If I weren't dying, it'd be oddly hot, but I'm dying, and this sucks. She grabs a fistful of my blood-soiled shirt and pulls me in. "A good IT girl always gets what she wants. It was never about River. It was about you."

She releases my shirt and my body slams to the floor of the stage.

Welp, I never thought I'd get stabbed, but there's a first time for everything. To squirt plasma from your neck like a crimson geyser. To bleed out. This is the end of the tragic comedy that is my life. The rafters above me are the long arms of the Grim Reaper, waiting to take me away.

When my grandmother had her near-death experience, she spoke of a tunnel with light. But I see no light. Oh, wait. My eyes are shut. I power them open. A cacophony of voices floods my ears. A "don't let her escape!" A "take her down." An "AC, you'll be fine."

The rafters sway.

So this is what it's like to get a visit from the Grim Reaper. Painfully ordinary, if you ask me. Or just painful, seeing as how a pen remains lodged in my neck.

I always thought dying would be scary. Not that getting stabbed in the neck isn't scary. But none of this scares me. Not in the classical, scaredy-cat sense. The lights. The ones my grandma told me about, they appear. They're not the ones in the rafters—these are different.

"AC, stay with us," a random voice pleads.

"Well, someone stop the bleeding!" someone shouts.

I've never seen or heard anything so clearly in my life. Funny how the end of life can do that you. My head turns. Everything is sideways. Like when I was a kid, my friends and I used to tell each other that's what we look like on earth because of gravity. Everything is 1080i quality video. Only better. The scuff marks on the woman's shoes from across the room, high definition. The Global Music Awards music-note ice sculpture melts, and the water drips slow enough for me to count each droplet...five...six...seven.

The blood trickling down my neck drips to the floor. Hot and syrupy. The drops are thunderous.

"AC, talk to me," says a pitched-down version of Cade. He's blurry. Too bad he showed up late.

"I'm sorry," I mutter.

"AC," mutters River in a quivery voice that makes me wanna find Lyla's pen and introduce it to his neck.

The lights disappear.

So here I lie, in a river of blood. *Because of River* is what the old AC would tell you. But this is not the old AC. This AC says he lies in a lake of blood because of AC.

"All clear!" shouts an EMT.

"He's gonna be okay, right?" Cade shouts. "Tell me he's gonna be okay!"

"AC, say something." I don't recognize the voice. Arms and hands fumble all over me. A surge of energy lights me up. I open my eyes again.

"Say something, dude," whimpers River, and I wish I had the strength to hurl myself up and ram my head into his little button nose.

What does he care if I live or die? Why does anyone care? Why do I care?

I lie in this river of blood with a clear vision of my life as it should be and my life as it is.

My tomb, as it stands now, will read: *Here lies the guy who failed at revenge. He lost the girl and got killed for his efforts.*

What a tragic legacy. A legacy of fake buffoonery. I have become the people I loathe.

"We're losing him," declares a frantic voice from a few feet away.

Nobody's losing anyone special is what I immediately think to myself.

"AC, buddy, wake up!" shouts a low-pitched voice to my right. Definitely Cade.

The other voice, the one that sounds like River's, sounds desperate. Miserable.

"I'm sorry for everything," says River.

Me, too.

"He's losing a lot of blood!" shouts a quivery voice.

Blood doesn't scare me, though. I remember Mom taking me to get a blood test when I was in high school. She would squirm as blood sprayed from my arm and into the tube. *"How can you people sleep at night?"* I would ask sarcastically.

"I'm gonna get sick," declares a monotone voice.

Everything sounds so...clear. Like an engineer from Bose hijacked my ears. Each gooey sound of someone moving about the blood-soaked floor. The smacking of sneaker sole and plasma. Each drop rolling off my neck and onto the floor.

I have well over a gallon of the stuff in my body, yet everyone around me acts as though I'm losing a tank of it.

"We have to stop the bleeding," shouts an unfamiliar voice. Probably an EMT.

"AC," whispers River, and I wish someone would hurry up and punch him in the trachea so he can't speak. "Stay strong, man."

His voice triggers a vision of his millions of fans. Fans likely ready to line up and wait patiently for hours so they have a chance to spit on my grave.

I see them in me. And me in them. Which explains why I'm here.

I rattle my head. I lift my arm to my face. It weighs a thousand pounds. I remove the oxygen mask and look at River, trying not to blink. "I can't wait to introduce your next shitty single on the radio," I say.

River grins.

"Well, let's try to convince Lilian to not fire you," says Cade.

"I don't care if she does," I mumble.

The last thing I hear is an EMT telling her colleague that I ruined her lunch break. That she was looking forward to grabbing a bite to eat from the newest taco truck. Something about Korean-Mexican fusion. Extra big burritos or something. And her buddy chimes in and tells her she can't handle anything Mexican. That the last time she had a burrito from a taco truck, she hurled all over her new Yeezys. I want to tell her that I know the feeling. But my eyes drag shut. And the curtain to this miserable chapter in my life fades to black.

CHAPTER 37

If you got this far without wanting me to fade away into the annals of bygone blowhards, then someone should give you a reward. A blue ribbon, maybe a trophy with a gold-plated plaque at the bottom that reads, "They tolerated a failure who failed so hard he couldn't even fail right." Or a medal with my face on it and a pen sticking out of my neck.

My mom once told me that Americans love to knock people down, just so they can lift them back up again.

But what if she's wrong?

What if Americans love to knock people down so they can have a metric for comparing their vapid lives? What if they canceled me so they don't have to cancel their own existence? So they can go and brag to their friends that "at least their life isn't as jacked up as that AC dude?"

These thoughts cloud my head as I stare at the reflection in my bathroom mirror. I dip a cotton swab into a small pool of hydrogen peroxide and run it along my neck. The ER doc said if the pen struck me a few more centimeters to the left, I would have died. Not exactly the most comforting thing to hear from a medical professional when you're strapped to a gurney and surrounded by strangers in scrubs. He also said it was kinda cool to see all that blood sputtering out like a fake murder victim from a low-budget horror movie. My pain, his gain.

I rip open the box of bandages next to the sink. They're decorated with My Little Pony because the drugstore down the street ran out of the nude-colored ones.

My neck is still sore to the touch, but the doctor told me there's no arterial damage and that I'd be making a full recovery.

Can't say the same for your career, he said.

He was right. The doctor usually is.

Management relieved me of my duties from Nexus Radio, and they pulled my syndicated show. Yep. They canceled the DJ.

And before you get excited about never having to listen to AC's voice talking over a River Bronswell track ever again, do this. Understand you'll never live rent-free in my head. So tweet the tweets, post the memes, and record the reaction videos on TikTok. Because I've decided to take all that negative energy, bottle it up, store it in my apartment, and consume when necessary. So please, keep it coming. I've learned to love my fate. Amor fati, bitches.

Before the Global Music Awards incident, people knew me as the puketastic loser who got dumped for River Bronswell.

And now, they'll know me as someone else. Someone who got his life together in an instant, made amends with the world's greatest musician, and reached the pinnacle of his career after languishing in the valley of despair.

Just kidding.

I'm radio kryptonite. River's people found out about the Ipecac. Lyla spilled all kinds of tea to the authorities. She used the Twitter spat with her brother as justification for nearly killing me. But I refused to press charges. She'd probably be declared innocent by reason of insanity if I did.

I dab a cotton swab along my neck and toss it into the wastebasket. I grab a bandage from the box, unwrap, and layer it on top of my neck. "*Hmph,*" I grumble to myself as I turn to the side and expose my neck for a better view.

My phone buzzes and dances about on the bathroom counter. Cade. *Be there in five minutes.*

In Cade's world, five minutes means two and a half minutes.

A T-shirt greets me from my bed. All black with white lettering. A gift from Cade. It reads, "River Bronswell stole my gf and all I got was stabbed in the neck (and this shirt)." I lift it over my head and pull it down over my body. Perfect fit. About three seconds into my self-admiration, the doorbell rings. My phone buzzes again. Cade.

I'm here, let me in.

As soon as my fingers type the words "door's open, let yourself in," he's in my apartment, standing with his hands on his hips in my living room.

"Why does your shirt look three sizes too small?" I ask.

He curls his upper lip. His shoulders bounce as he chuckles. "Because you eat too much soy, and I work out three times harder than you." He flexes his pecs. They twitch from inside his shirt like puppies trying to escape a throw blanket. "Bet you can't do that with your moobs."

"Don't make me cancel you for targeted harassment of my underdeveloped pecs," I reply, heading to the kitchen. "Bottle of water?"

"Nah," he says, examining the microphones set up in my living room. One in front of my leather chair, and the other in front of the love seat. "Setup looks great, if you forget the fact that the cords are worming all over the floor."

"Well, good thing nobody sees the floor since it's a podcast, and the video footage won't be recording the floor. Brainiac."

Cade plops himself down on my couch. He rests an arm on his knee and asks, "So, how is the podcast coming along?"

"Meh." I shrug. "Without the institutional backing of the Nexus Radio machine, subpar at best."

"Sorry dude," he says.

"Don't be," I say. "It'll take off. Eventually."

"True."

"So what movie are we watching?"

Cade's lips part, then close. His Adam's apple pulses, and he looks up at the ceiling. "Aubrey."

I grab a seat on the chair across from him. "You calling me 'Aubrey' always leads to unpleasant things."

"Frogs and dinosaurs, Aubrey," he says. He gets up and paces around my apartment. The slightly older brother I never had gives me an impromptu TED Talk.

Blah blah blah, frogs survived the gigantic asteroid that plowed into Earth and killed off the dinosaurs all those millions of years ago. *Blah blah blah*, you can choose how to react to every proverbial asteroid that hits your world. *Blah blah blah* so be like Kermit. Not like Barney.

I shift myself in my chair. The sun beams through the living room and down on his head. My eyes squint shut from the shimmer. "What does the movie we're gonna watch have to do with frogs and dinosaurs?"

Cade stops behind me and slaps a hand on my shoulder. "Today, you and I are going to run an exercise in exposing ourselves to something we find repulsive." He lays down two large tickets on the armrest of my chair.

The tickets show Miles Teller, Cara Delevingne, and Cole Sprouse. Miles and Cara stand back-to-back. Her arms are crossed. He holds a ukelele, the sound hole covers Kurt Cobain's face and the "i" and "r" on his Nirvana concert T-shirt. She's wearing a ball cap with a braid bleeding downward out the back, yoga pants, and a baseball-style jersey with River's face on it. Headphones wrap around Cole's neck. In his hand is a bottle labeled with a skull and crossbones.

"No," I growl, crossing my arms.

"Frog or dinosaur?"

I look down at the tickets. Above Miles, Cara, and Cole is the word "Inebriated." Underneath, the subtitle reads, "Inspired by the WattPad original, based on actual events."

I slap the tickets on my coffee table, and now my life is worse than a meme that lives for fifteen minutes on the internet.

Cade and I lock eyes. He breaks the staredown and glances at the tickets. "Sources say the book is better."

"Sources say if I had the money, I'd spend an entire paycheck on Bobbi's fanfic, light a bonfire with it, and mail the ashes to her place."

"Just a tad aggressive," he replies.

He's right.

"Fine," I say. "Let's go. I haven't been to a movie theater since pre-COVID anyway."

Ninety-nine percent of us will be forgotten in ninety-nine years. And ninety-nine percent of the world will never know of this unfortunate turn of events. Which means most of the world will never know my memetastically pathetic life inspired a movie. Awesome.

Now excuse me, I've gotta go and amor some fati.